Ten-four
good buddy, ten-four!
Roll the channels,
Modulate...

ELECTRA—The husky voice that lends the high-school boys a helping hand.

PAPA THERMODYNE—Lost on roads long gone.

HOT COFFEE—Her business is mobile.

THE CHROME ANGEL—With more wives than he can handle.

BLOOD—The voice that's after Spider.

SPIDER—CB purist and crusader, the Dudley Doright of the airwaves.

PLUS a wild cast of fantastic wavejammers who add up to action, romance, excitement, and good truckin'

on

CITIZENS
BAND

PARAMOUNT PICTURES PRESENTS

CITIZENS BAND

PAUL LE MAT
CANDY CLARK
ANN WEDGEWORTH
MARCIA RODD
CHARLES NAPIER

Music by
BILL CONTI

Associate Producer
PAUL BRICKMAN

Executive Producer
SHEP FIELDS

Written by
PAUL BRICKMAN

Directed by
JONATHAN DEMME

A FIELDS COMPANY PRODUCTION
A PARAMOUNT PICTURE

CITIZENS BAND

Novelization by
E. M. Corder

From a screenplay by
Paul Brickman

A KANGAROO BOOK
PUBLISHED BY POCKET BOOKS NEW YORK

CITIZENS BAND

POCKET BOOK edition published May, 1977

This original POCKET BOOK edition is printed from brand-new
plates made from newly set, clear, easy-to-read type.
POCKET BOOK editions are published by
POCKET BOOKS,
a Simon & Schuster Division of
GULF & WESTERN CORPORATION
1230 Avenue of the Americas,
New York, N.Y. 10020.
Trademarks registered in the United States
and other countries.

_____

ISBN: 0-671-81180-0.

Printed in the U.S.A.

CHAPTER 1

THE BIG HEAVY OLDSMOBILE MOVED SOFTLY through the cold, late March rain, its engine thrumming lowly. The swish of the windshield wipers was rhythmic and monotonous. Behind the wheel, Richie Webber, sixteen and breathing shallowly, chewed on his lower lip.

The lancing headlights picked out an old pickup truck parked at the side of the dark back-country road. The pickup's exhaust pipe issued a steady small cloud of steam. The windows were vaporized on the inside, masking its occupants from sight.

A few feet further on, a red Dodge was parked, and a little past that a peppy little Pinto. Their windows were also fogged, engines barely audible over the thrum of Richie's own. Ahead, the vague shapes of other cars could dimly be seen, an occasional flare of a safety reflector or glint from a piece of chrome.

Courteously, Richie cut his headlights down to parking lights. Sometimes—not often, but sometimes—deputies from the county sheriff's department decided to roll through this lover's lane to raise a little anxiety in behalf of the grown-ups' dedicated commitment to chastity. Teen-age chastity, anyway. So when lights flared through the steamy windows of the parked cars, couples would spring apart in panic, adjusting clothes, smearing lipstick off their mouths, running frantic fingers through their hair trying to straighten it. It was polite to reassure your comrades by cutting your lights as soon as you came upon their cars. The deputies only did this when they were feeling particularly mean and low-down or when they had a mad on against some certain kid they wanted to nail.

Richie found an empty spot and pulled the Olds over, killing the parking lights. His throat became dry. He felt like his lips were cracking and he licked them. He leaned back, closed his eyes, and listened to the last stanza of the song on the radio. It was a girl, lamenting the fact that she hadn't given her boyfriend "that little bit of lovin' that was all he asked" before he took his big Harley out on the racetrack to try to win the money to buy her an engagement ring with. He died in a flaming crash, and they buried him "without that little bit of lovin' that was all he asked."

Oh, yeah. Oh, yeah. She was so sorry. Richie could almost forgive her. He heard every girl who'd ever turned him down singing the song to him. Oh, yeah. He was so sad, he could almost forgive them.

Richie hardly ever came here. Because he could hardly ever get his girl, Karen (or any other), to come with him. His complexion was getting worse by the day. Oh, yeah. It was so sad.

The song ended. He turned off the radio and switched on the CB bracket-mounted under the dash. Sweat sprang to his palms. A lump grew in his throat. He swallowed several times. He didn't want his voice to break or choke off.

He turned the channel selector to Five. His legs trembled. He was suddenly very warm. He turned off the heater's blower.

He compressed his lips, keyed the mike. He was paralyzed a moment, then he forced himself to speak.

"How 'bout it, Electra, you out there?"

Pam Armbruster turned off the shower handles, slid back the glass door, and stepped out of her tub onto the bath mat. She took a big fluffy towel from the ring, held both ends and flipped it over her shoulders, and began drying her back. She was tall and supple-bodied, in her early twenties. Her breasts were high and they yearned upward and outward. Her nipples were cherry red and puckered from the cold water she'd finished her shower with. She ran the towel down the swan's-neck curve of her back, roughed the creamy surface of her saucy buttocks with it, dried the long, strong, slender willowiness of her legs. She rubbed a circle in the vapored mirror with her towel, hooked her shower cap with her thumbs, and flipped it off, letting it fall to the floor. She shook her head, which loosened a cascade of soft wavy chestnut hair to fall about her shoulders.

She winked at herself in the mirror and gave a sexy little bump of her hips for no reason other than that she felt good. Pam Armbruster liked herself—not with outrageous egotism, but healthily so. And justifiably, for she was pretty, intelligent, and had a dynamite body.

The CB set on the little marble-topped table next to the bed in her bedroom crackled through the partly open door.

"How 'bout it, Electra, you out there?"

Pam knotted the towel around herself, stepped from the bathroom, crossed the bedroom, bounced onto the bed, and picked the mike off its hook.

"This is Electra," she said. "Come on." She made her voice much lower and more velvety than it normally was.

"This here's the Warlock," answered the voice. "Do you copy?"

Pam glanced at the indicator.

"I'm getting about eight pounds. Come on."

"I just wondered if I was getting out with this storm and all."

"I read you wall to wall. What did you say your handle was?"

"Warlock."

"What's your twenty, Warlock?"

"Hampton Park. What's yours?"

"You know I can't tell you that."

"Are you on a base or a mobile?"

"Can't tell you that either."

"Do you know the Leprechaun?"

Pam scrunched up her forehead, looking for the handle. "Who?"

"The Leprechaun. He was with you last week."

"Oh, him! He was very sexy. Do you know him?"

"He's my best friend. Say, do you go to school around here?"

"Hey, I can't give out all my secrets, can I? Did the Leprechaun tell you to call me?"

"Yeah."

"Are you . . . alone?" Pam asked softly.

"Yeah."

"That's nice. Why don't you take off your jacket and get more comfortable?"

"Uh, my jacket?" Warlock answered with some agitation.

"Mmm-hmmm," Pam purred.

"Ten-four," Warlock said breathily.

Pam waited a beat, then said, "There, that's better, isn't it?"

"Yeah."

Pam picked a brush from next to the CB on the night table. She began pulling it slowly through the shining waves of her hair.

"There are a lot of voices out there," she said quietly, "but yours is different. I like it. What are you wearing?"

"Jeans and . . . a shirt."

Pam smiled. "What kind of shirt?"

"Uh, flannel."

"Undershirt?"

"No."

"That's nice. Flannel is soft and warm against the skin, don't you think?"

"Uh-huh."

"Do you mind if I slide my hand under your shirt? My hand is soft and warm too."

She could hear him take breath sharply. "No," he said. "No, I don't mind."

"Now just let me open a couple of buttons and . . . there. Oh! You feel so nice and muscular. Are you on a team?"

"Basketball."

"You feel so nice. Do you feel my hand? I'm rubbing it ever so softly over your skin. Do you feel me?"

"Uh . . . I think so . . ."

"Well, I sure feel you. Oh, yes, I do. Oh, yes."

On the northbound highway, approaching Union, Harold Rissley gripped the wheel of his big, cattle-hauling eighteen-wheeler and squinted past the beating wipers through the heavy rain to the taillights of the dark sedan ahead of him, which was moving a little too boldly through the storm. Well, hell, that was the civvie's lookout. Harold had to make time, and, though it perked his alertness, rain didn't bother him any, and he was grateful he hadn't been stuck behind some little old lady crawling at a money-eating ten per hour.

He fished a cigarette out of his pocket, stuck it in his lips, picked a throwaway butane lighter from the dash tray, and flicked the flame to life.

He dropped his eyes a fraction of a second to line the flame up with the cigarette. When he looked up again he blurted, "Jesus Christ!" He spat the cigarette away, dropped the lighter, and grabbed the wheel with both hands again and yanked it sideways.

The sedan had clipped the shoulder. It yawed across the road, the brake lights flared, and then it went spinning round and round.

"Oh, Mama!" Harold moaned.

He jerked the wheel harder. He didn't have any

choice. It was that or climb up right over the sedan and make it scrap metal.

The high blunt-nosed cab veered to the side. The heavy trailer whipped after it. The weight and momentum took control and the rig jack-knifed onto the shoulder. Harold stood on the brakes. The compressed air blasted. The cab bounced and slued, snapped Harold about, then came to a halt.

"Phew!" Harold released his pent breath in a burst.

Through the curtain of rain, he saw the driver of the sedan bring his vehicle back under control, touch his brakes hesitantly, as if glancing back at Harold through his rearview mirror, then get off the brakes and speed up, disappearing into the night.

"Thanks," Harold muttered. "You're a scholar and a gentleman."

He hit the switch for his emergency flashers, reached behind him into the bunk for his jacket. He shrugged into it and stepped out into the storm, jumping down, holding the jacket closed with his hand.

"Aw, shit," he said.

The wheels of the right side were buried in mud. There was no way out.

The cattle in his load were bawling and banging about.

"Calm down," he said, "you ain't hamburger yet."

He got back into the cab and turned the CB channel selector to Nine, keyed the mike.

Spider Lovejoy—actually, it was Blaine Love-joy, but that was one of the worst names he'd ever heard, even if it was his own—sat on a stool before his workbench in the wood and tarpaper structure out behind the house that was his workshop. He'd been tagged "Spider" when he was a skinny leggy kid. He wasn't skinny or leggy anymore (he was lean and muscular, and square-jawed and handsome to boot, and in the bloom of his middle twenties), but he liked the nickname and he'd kept it. He'd even had a spider web stenciled onto his T-shirts, one of which he was wearing now. The raw insulation tacked to the unfinished walls and the wood stove crackling in the corner kept the workshop shirt-sleeve comfortable through all but the fiercest winter weather.

CB units—assembled and disassembled—were strewn across his workbench along with meters, boxes of capacitors and relays, tuning pots, wire, soldering irons, and a variety of other science-fiction film gadgets.

Spider squinted in concentration as he worked on a juncture with thin needle-nose pliers and a Lilliputian jeweler's screwdriver.

A voice crackled out of his own, personal base station, which was tuned to the emergency channel.

"React Monitor! React Monitor! This is the Chrome Angel KHD4432, Over."

Spider dropped his tools for the mike. "This is KKT6757, Union React. Go ahead, Chrome Angel."

"Well, gracious sakes alive, React. Terrible cottonpickin' thing. Doggone four-wheeler blew my rig off the road. Mercy. You got a wrecker out there or something? Terrible cottonpickin' thing."

"Ten-four, Chrome Angel. What's your twenty?"

"Highway Seventy-three. Northbound. A little past the Reddin exit."

"How 'bout a mile marker?"

"Mercy. That's a negatory."

"Stand by a minute. Chrome Angel." Spider switched channels. "This is Union React to Texaco Jack. Come on." He paused. "This is Union React to Texaco Jack. How 'bout it?"

"Hey, Hustler," a boy's voice said, "did you see Margie Frankel at the dance?"

"Yeah, this is the Hustler," another boy answered. "She's a fox, a total fox."

"Break!" Spider said in annoyance.

"But she's sixteen and always on the rag," the Hustler said.

"Break! Break!" Spider said into the mike. "You're in violation of FCC regulation 95:41. Channel Nine is reserved for emergency use only."

"Hey, Hustler," the first boy said. "Take it to Twenty."

"Ten-four," the Hustler said.

"This is Union React to Texaco Jack," Spider said. "How 'bout it?"

A mile and a half away, on another rainswept highway, the night was lit with bright red flares and glaring spotlights. In the center of this were six cars slanted across the highway, battered and crumpled, one on its top, another smoldering beneath its ruptured hood. Two wreckers stood nearby, one with its winch chain hooked to the rear axle of a twisted Pontiac. A pair of state troopers stood off to the side writing in notebooks. A handful of men in down parkas and bulky plaid wool jackets were working with pry bars, trying to separate two of the cars.

Through the open window of the biggest wrecker, a bright blue GMC brute of a machine, came a CB call.

"This is Union React to Texaco Jack. How 'bout it?"

A big man with a baseball cap on his head, his dense black beard soaked with rain, set down his pry bar, loped over to the wrecker, and reached his hand in for the mike.

"Go, React," he said. "Is that you, Spider?"

"Roger. We got an eighteen-wheeler off the road near the Reddin ramp. Requests assistance."

The big man shook his head. "Negative, Spider. I got a six-car TA here that's a real gooey mess. Looks like we'll be pullin' things unstuck for another hour or so. Back to ya."

"Ten-four there, Texaco Jack. You go right ahead with your TA and don't let the rain getcha under. Thank you for the comeback. This is KKT6757, Union React. We're clear."

Harold got a couple of flat rocks and pressed them down into the mud beneath the coupling between the tractor and the trailer, then positioned his hydraulic jack on them and pumped the jack up, trying to lift the mired wheels free so he could put something under them for traction.

The wheels lifted slowly. The wind howled and slashed a sheet of rain against the truck. The cattle moaned, panicked, and shifted violently. Their moving weight unbalanced the trailer, and it slipped the jack and fell, pinning Harold's arm between a support strut and the coupling.

He threw back his head and screamed.

Spider sighed. A six-car pile-up meant that all the service station guys in town were there, or on the way.

A heavy fist banged on the door.

"C'mon in," Spider called. "It's open."

The door swung in, funneling a blast of cold rain. Spider shivered. A great thyroidal hulk of a young man entered, slamming the door closed behind him. He stamped the mud and water from his boots. The heavy wrapping around his body ballooned him even larger than the 300 pounds he weighed. He unwrapped a muffler from around his face, exposing its broad, ruddy, but angelically innocent, features.

"Hey, good buddy," Spider greeted.

"Hey!" Cochise responded.

His voice was high and reedy. A vast grin widened his mouth. He held up an impressively large, but as yet unfinished, model airplane.

Spider grinned back. "Just a minute," he said.

He turned his CB back to the emergency channel.

"This is Union React to KHD4432."

Cochise set his model down carefully on the end of Spider's workbench. He shrugged out of his coat and hung it on a nail protruding from one of the raw studs. He removed his leather cap from his head, lifting it by the furry ear flaps.

"This is Union React to that Chrome Angel. Do you copy?"

There was only low-level static. Spider frowned.

"Negative copy on that KHD4432 caught in a drift," he broadcast. "This is KKT6757 Union

React going ten-ten, ten-eight, and monitoring."

Spider sat scratching his head. Then he turned on his stool, pulled on his boots. He picked his jacket from over the back of a chair.

"Cochise, how would you like to take over the base for a little while? I got a gear jockey stuck on Seventy-three and I can't raise him."

Cochise's eyes lit up. "Sure, Spider!"

"You just sit here and watch over things."

"You bet! You don't have to worry about anything! Can I have a Coke?"

"Sure, get one from the fridge." Spider inclined his head toward a beat-up old refrigerator in the corner. "Just sit here and watch over things, okay?"

"Sure!"

Spider nodded at the model. "How's it coming?"

Cochise turned the model in his hands. The wing-span was longer than Spider's arms. It was made of canvas and delicately carved wood. Cochise moved a small lever in the cockpit. A tiny motor whirred and the tail rudder moved from side to side. He shifted a second lever. Another motor engaged, and the wing flaps shifted up and down.

"Lookin' good," Spider said.

Cochise's smile broadened to the point where it threatened to run over past the sides of his face. He bobbed his head in pleasure.

Snap!

One of the wing flaps descended too far, broke at the joint, and fell to the floor.

Cochise's smile faded.

Spider shook his head. "Umph. Needs fixing, good buddy."

"No sweat." Cochise's smile returned.

"You bet," Spider said.

Then he went out the door and into the blustery night.

CHAPTER 2

WITH THE MIKE IN HER HAND, PAM ROLLED BACK on her spine, pulled a delicious pair of white net panties up her legs, then arched her pelvis and snugged them around her hips. She rocked back up, sat cross-legged, and reached for her sweater.

"Come on. . . ." Warlock said.

"I'm taking off my sweater now," Pam purred into the mike, doing just the opposite. "Would you be more comfortable in the back?"

"No, I'm okay," Warlock answered eagerly.

"What are you taking off?" Pam inquired, straightening her sweater, and taking up a faded pair of embroidered blue jeans.

"What do you want me to take off?" Warlock squeaked.

Pam stood up from the bed, stepped into her jeans, and pulled them up with one hand. "Why don't we start by loosening your belt buckle a bit?"

"Sure," he rasped.

"You're not nervous, are you?"

"N-no."

"Good. Because I'm taking off the rest now. Just let me unfasten my skirt . . . there. And now the last of it . . . there. . . . This is how I look. . . . Do you like me?"

"Uh, you're beautiful."

"I'm a little shy about this birthmark. This one right here, on the inside of my thigh. Do you see it?"

"Where? Where?" he said hoarsely.

"Right . . . here. Let me put your hand on it. That's it. You won't make fun of it, will you?"

"Of course not," he promised.

"Can we loosen your jeans a little more? I'd like to touch you. You can touch me too. My hands aren't too cold, are they?"

"No . . . no . . . oh, no, they're not!"

"Oooohh," Pam moaned. "You feel so nice. Do you feel me?"

"Oh, yes!" he said quaveringly.

Pam took a nail file from the night table and began to dress up her toenails. "Oh, Warlock," she murmured. "Now I'm going to . . ."

Spider's wheels were a '56 Chevy Nomad that he'd painstakingly and lovingly rebuilt himself. Spider had a way with machines—the way other people do with animals or children. Spider understood them, and, weirdly, they seemed to appreciate and respond to that understanding. Where other men would sweat and curse for half an hour trying to loosen a frozen nut, it seemed to drop at the touch of Spider's fingers. Clogged gas-lines would magically clear themselves. Burnt-out resistors would summon his eye. . . .

The roads he took to reach Highway 73 and the marooned Chrome Angel were dark and rain-whipped. He tried raising the trucker on the CB again, but couldn't. He didn't like it. It was flukey.

He turned onto the highway and picked out the canted silhouette of the truck five minutes later. He pulled carefully to a stop behind it, turned on his emergency flashers, picked a couple of flares from beneath the seat, and got out.

He struck the first flare and planted it behind the truck, walked on up to the front and ignited and positioned the second flare and walked back. He climbed up on the cab's step and rapped on the window.

"Hello?"

He didn't see anyone.

"Hello?"

He opened the door and peered in, frowning. He got down, cupped his hands and called, but no one answered. He walked around the truck.

"Holy Jesus!" he said. Harold was slumped over unconscious, held partly upright by his trapped arm.

Spider jumped forward, re-set the jack, and pumped like a madman. The trailer lifted slowly, groaning, and the frightened cattle bawled.

A truck pulled off the road just ahead of Harold's. The driver got out, shielding his eyes against the rain with his hand, saw what was happening, jumped down and came running back.

Spider had enough play between the coupling and the strut to ease Harold loose. Spider was sweating.

"What can I do?" the new driver said.

"Get an ambulance. He's lost blood."

Spider ran back to the Nomad and broke out a blanket, first-aid kit, and a small oxygen unit from the trunk.

The other trucker was back with Harold, cradling Harold's head in his lap. "They said it'd be another ten minutes before they can get here."

Spider tied off Harold's arm with a tourniquet, then put the oxygen mask over his face. "Breathe," he said anxiously. "Breathe."

He lifted the mask after a few moments. There was the thinnest whistle of air through Harold's nostrils. Spider replaced the mask.

"Come on, guy! Breathe!"

After a tense minute, Harold's hand fluttered up and weakly pushed aside the mask. His eyes opened and rolled in aimless circles.

"Terrible . . . cottonpickin' . . . thing," he said.

Pam had moved to her dressing table. It was awkward trying to get her eye makeup right with just one hand, but it was kind of fun too, and she wouldn't think of letting Warlock down. All those poor horny kids going out of their minds with frustration. Grown-up society treated them horribly, conspiring with perverse nastiness to suppress their urges and fill them with guilt at precisely the time in their lives when their juices flowed most copiously and their bodies ached with forbidden desire. Pam felt great sympathy toward adolescents. She saw them every day, and she saw their agonies. She wondered sometimes if she were doing this in compensation for her own childhood, which had been terrible and abusive, or for the sake of the kids she'd grown up with. She remembered the fears and doubts and unhappiness of her friends vividly, and she'd promised herself, at one particularly miserable point in her young life, never to forget what it was like when she grew older, to try to understand and sympathize with the ones who came after her.

Well, whatever the reason, it was harmless at the worst, and at the best could bring some happiness into the world.

"Warlock?" she gasped into the mike.

"Yeah?" he groaned.

"Don't stop. Don't ever stop."

"I won't. . . ."

"Oh!" she said. "It's never been this good before!"

"I know. . . ."

"Oh, gosh, keep going. Hurry . . . yes . . . please . . . oh! . . ."

"Yes . . . yes . . ."

"Oh, I can't stand it!" Pam said, fingertipping a dab of perfume behind each ear. "I'm going to explode . . . hurry . . . please . . ."

"Oh, yes . . ."

A new, unfamiliar voice crashed in on them, like a stone through a windowpane.

"Break. Break."

"Oh, God!" Warlock wailed. "Please, wait. . . ."

"How 'bout it, Moondog?" the intruder asked. "You out there for the Nightmare?"

"Warlock?" Pam said.

"I said, how 'bout it, Moondog? You out there?"

"Warlock?"

Nightmare said, "Uh, negative copy on that break. We gone."

There was static.

"Warlock?" Pam asked softly.

Several seconds of empty silence passed. Then Warlock, despair in his voice, said, "Yeah."

"Are you okay?"

"Yeah," he answered dully.

"I'm sorry about that breaker," Pam whispered.

"That's all right."

"Can we start again?"

"I can't," Warlock said bitterly. "It's ruined."

Pam's heart went out to the poor kid, the fragile ego of his age.

"Maybe you can come back another night," she said.

"Sure. . . . Hey, uh, listen. I'm in my father's car and I was supposed to get it back and everything, so maybe I better back off and go ten-seven."

She imagined his discomfort, not knowing what to say to her.

"Will you call again?" she asked. "I really like your voice."

"Uh-huh," he said. "Well, ten-four. We're clear."

The channel went to static.

Pam made a rueful face into her mirror. Poor Warlock.

CHAPTER 3

THE TINY LITTLE FARMHOUSE, WHICH LOOKED like something a wealthy farmer might build for his children, sat bleakly off to the side of the road that looped around Union. The roof was missing shingles, half the verandah had rotted out and collapsed, and the paint was peeling. The barn, off to the side, was big enough, but excepting a big handpainted scrawl in bright red enamel, it hadn't seen paint in years. The scrawl said: THE FUNNY FARM—REST HOME FOR A RETIRED TRUCKER. Lower, in smaller script, were the words, *CB Radios Repaired*. About half the boards were missing, having been used by Floyd Lovejoy for firewood. Spider was always wanting to cut and chop firewood from the old dead timber stand out back. He said the barn was too pretty to tear down. Floyd couldn't see what was pretty about an old barn. He didn't give a damn how much firewood Spider cut. The boy could chop and split till he was blue in the face as far as Floyd was concerned, but that didn't stop Floyd from tearing off the boards as the mood took him. It pained him to see all that good seasoned burning stuff just sitting there nailed to that framework doing nothing.

Scattered about and around the Funny Farm were the behemoth carcasses of old rusted, battered, worn-out trucks. They sat on flattened and rotted tires. They leaned, they tilted, some were half sunk into the soil. Oxidized parts lay strewn everywhere. It looked the site of an old battleground that no one had bothered to clean up.

Spider was in the kitchen, which overlooked his tarpaper workshop out back. The storm was over and the sun was out, but drops from a residual puddle of water on the roof were falling from the eaves past the window, to strike annoyingly on an old piece of tin resting up against the side of the house.

Ping. Ping-ping. Ping.

Spider pulled a can of Mighty Dog from the cabinet, put the opener to it, and pressed down. As the lid was punctured, a stench that would have gagged a ghoul burst out with a hiss. Spider snapped his head away.

"Yaaaach," he said, repulsed.

It was the cheapest dog food at the market, but Ned seemed to thrive on it; in fact, he positively seemed to love it. Sometimes Spider thought the dog was half pig.

He turned his face to the side and breathed through his mouth while he dug the stuff out with a spoon into an old teeth-pocked plastic bowl.

"No wonder you smell like shit," he said to Ned.

Ned the Dog sat at Spider's feet looking up in anticipation. He was part collie, part husky, part cocker spaniel (and probably part pig and part sphinx, and part four dozen other things too). His shoulder was about as high as Spider's knee. His body, beneath a coat that would have done a yak proud, was long and skinny. His legs were way too long, he had one brown eye and one blue one, and he had a manner of walking that would have made Charlie Chaplin green with envy. His breath smelled like rotten eggs and goat cheese.

His tufted tail thumped the floor in slow, lethargic rhythm while Spider filled the bowl.

Whack . . . whack . . . whack.

Spider put the bowl down in the corner.

Ned got up and walked over to it, each of his legs seeming to go in a different direction, his body yawing from side to side.

Once he got up momentum, Ned frequently became enchanted with the idea, and often forgot what had started it all. This time he walked right past his food (over it, actually), wagging his tail in that weird stop-action way of his. He stopped when his left rear paw came down in the center of his putrid fare.

He stood still, trying to reason his way through the foreign gooeyness in which he stood.

"Good, Ned," Spider said. "Real good."

Ned looked up. His face brightened. He loved being praised by Spider.

Then he turned his head and studied his foot. After a moment's reflection, he lifted it up, standing on three legs.

"Smart doggie," Spider said.

Ned swished his tail.

Ned paused, developing a plan, then put it into action. First, he shook his foot. Second, he lowered it back down to the worn linoleum. Third, he turned around. His head was now over his food bowl. He looked up at Spider for approval.

"Wonderful," Spider said.

Ned pulled his lips back over his brown teeth in a grotesque smile. Then he dipped his head and grabbed a mouthful of the reeking meat-mash with a little shiver of delight.

Shaking his head, Spider took a corn flakes box from the Kellogg's Variety Pak in the cupboard. The cupboard was old and had glass doors that had been painted over. Everything in the dim slope-floored kitchen had been painted over, but that didn't make it look any less dingy.

"Pop," he called.

Floyd Lovejoy shambled into the kitchen, wiping his hands on a bath towel. He tossed the towel onto the back of a chair. It fell off to the floor. Floyd didn't notice, or didn't care. He sat down at the fuchsia and white dinette, with gold flakes, put his elbows on the top, and cupped his jaw in his hands.

Spider put a bowl and a spoon and the corn flakes box in front of him.

Floyd looked down at them with neither interest nor lack of it.

Floyd was sixty-four, but looked ten years older. His stiff crew-cut had grayed, then gone to white a long time ago. His shoulders were rounded. His hands were knobby and freckled on the back. The old tattoos on his veiny arms had faded, as if in sympathy with his general malaise.

The only thing that seemed to prick his consciousness at all were the vague sounds of distant voices from his CB set, which was within reach on an old lamp table behind him. Spider's own set, tuned to Channel Nine, the emergency channel, was on the counter at the other end of the table.

Spider opened the corn flakes and poured them into his father's bowl. Floyd watched without response. Spider poured milk over the cereal, then pushed the sugar bowl over. Floyd dully spooned sugar onto the cereal. Spider filled a bowl for himself. The toast popped up. He buttered it, gave one slice to his father and one to himself, which he set directly on the table next to his bowl. He poured coffee for them both.

"How're you feeling?" he asked.

Floyd chewed his first mouthful, thought about it a moment after he swallowed, then dumped on another spoonful of sugar.

"Okay," he said.

"Good."

They ate in silence.

Floyd's CB set crackled to life: "Hey, Papa Thermodyne—this here's Duddly Doright! You got your ears on today?"

Life flared into Floyd's eyes and he jumped his chair around to face the se "Well, doggone it, Duddly Doright, I didn't 'spec you for another day, that's fer sure, fer sure. You must be keepin' the hammer down to that ol' super-slab!"

"Yeah, well ten-four, good buddy. 'Bout that hammer, with all that storm—"

Another voice bled into the channel, souring Floyd's face: "The Lord must've been running linears the other night 'cause, mercy sakes, I never seen such talk power. That's the thing about

Jesus. You don't need no ears to catch his signal. Now give the Priest a big ol' four on that."

Spider grabbed the mike from Floyd. "Hey, Priest, whoever you are—you're walkin' all over a nice old man who's trying to modulate with a friend and that's damn rude."

Static sounded.

"Duddly, you still there?" Spider asked.

"Go," Duddly said.

Spider handed the mike back to his father.

Floyd perked up again. "Hey," he broadcast, "you say how-do to all my boys at K&L when you hit the Dirty Side, all right? And tell those cotton-pickin' cowboys to give me a shout when they pass the ol' Funny Farm. By golly, ain't nothin' perk up this lonely ol' sidewinder like talkin' with my boys!"

"Hey, that's a big ol' ten-four there. I'll certainly do that fer sure. You stay close to that rig and we'll modulate with you on the flip side. We down."

"Mercy, thanks for the shout. Keep the Dirty Side down and the Shiny Side up! Mercy!"

Floyd sat beaming at his set. Slowly his smile faded. When he turned back to the table his face was gray and empty. He picked up his spoon and began lifting cereal into his mouth again.

Spider took a bite of toast, chewed, swallowed. "How'd you sleep last night?" he asked.

Floyd shrugged. "Okay."

Silence settled again.

Spider rummaged through a box of electronics parts.

Spider finished before Floyd, who, eating being one of the few activities left in the dusty box of his life, spent a lot of time over it.

"I'm going out to the workshop a minute," Spider said.

"Okay."

Floyd slumped alone in the kitchen, carefully and slowly loading his spoon and lifting it to his mouth. He paused and lifted his head slightly.

"What stinks around here?" he mumbled to himself.

There was a *huff-huff-huff* at his knee.

He looked down.

Ned the Dog sat there with eyes half closed, panting away.

"Oh," Floyd said.

He reached into his pocket, extracted a Binaca spray, and blasted a jet into Ned's mouth.

The dog yelped and jumped back, and gave Floyd a series of sharp little querulous barks.

"Don't go breathin' on me, moose breath," Floyd said with a self-satisfied chortle.

Spider held up a microphone.

"Pop, I got you a new mike. You said the old one made your arm tired. See how this one feels."

Floyd, who had managed finally to finish his breakfast, tipped his cup and sipped the last of the coffee out, then turned his chair around to face his set. A bottle of Old Crow stood next to it. He poured a slug into the empty coffee cup and downed it, wiping his arm across his mouth with a grunt.

Spider hooked up the mike.

"How's that?" he asked. "See, it sets on the table so you don't have to hold it."

Floyd nodded. "Okay."

"If it doesn't work out, we'll see about getting you another one."

"Okay."

"Good. You're all set up now. I gotta go to town today. There's some wieners in the frig. And I left your toasted marshmallows next to the Ding-Dongs. Anything I can get you?"

Floyd turned his furrowed, slack face. "Take the dog," he said sepulchrally.

"I can't, Dad. I got a lot to do."

"Then the dog dies."

"C'mon, Dad. . . ."

"The dog dies."

Spider's Nomad rolled toward town smooth as a water drop down an icicle. The dozen CB sets with the red repair tags wired to them were in the trunk, separated with pieces of corrugated cardboard and wrapped around with several thicknesses of old tattered blankets to cushion them against jolting. It was still a little chilly outside, but Spider had his window rolled partway down.

Against the poisonous fumes that issued from Ned's mouth.

Ned was in the back seat. He liked the breeze. He hunched forward, his nose nearly pressing against Spider's neck, breathing deeply of the clean country air.

Unfortunately, Ned was in favor of breathing through his mouth.

Spider was now breathing through his own mouth in self-defense.

The sprightly old woman's voice kept on from his CB with no sign of flagging energy.

"That summer, it was '26, the family was all together," she said. "We were enjoying the little ones in the new house. That was also the summer I met Tom. He was delivering ice—remember those days?—and I was caring for the petunias.

Well, I got some water on him and one thing led
to another and the next thing I knew he was chas-
ing me around the garage . . ."

Spider angled the car over to the shoulder and
pulled to a stop.

"Well, I was a pretty sprightly runner in those
days, but for some reason, I didn't feel speedy
that day . . ."

Spider rolled his window up, leaned over, and
lowered the passenger window a little. He rapped
his knuckles on the pane.

"Here, boy. Here. Much better air on this side.
You'll love it."

Ned shifted over. He thumped his tail and stuck
his nose to the crack.

"Good boy," Spider said with relief.

He put the car in gear and took off.

"Now Tom had a pair of shoulders like a
lumberjack," the old lady said, "and a glint in
his eye that was brighter than a star . . ."

A masculine voice came over hers with a crackling "Good gracious! I think the old motormouth's
tellin' her life story!"

A second voice replied, "She's been jack-jawin'
for two days straight and she's still got another
sixty years to tell."

"Somebody ought to run down and drop a bottle
of Sominex in her Ovaltine," the first man said.
"That'd get the channel rollin' again. Good gracious!"

Texaco Jack' big wrecker pulled slowly into
his station, towing Harold's disabled Kenworth
like a dead whale. The fenders and sides were
splattered with mud. The rest of the truck,
heavy with chrome accouterments, gleamed in

faultless testament to long, loving hours of work. Painted in flowery script on the driver's door were the words CHROME ANGEL, and beneath that, HAROLD RISSLEY.

Harold, his left arm in a fresh plaster cast, was in the wrecker's cab with Texaco Jack. He watched with grudging admiration as Jack maneuvered the truck up alongside the fence. They got out together.

At the gas pumps, Cochise gave change to a customer, then came over to scrunch down and peer under the truck with them.

Jack pointed. "Looks bent over there."

"Must've hit a rock," Harold said glumly.

"Must've," Jack said. "Bent here too."

"Could've been the guard rail."

"Could've. Your lines are broken too."

Harold sighed.

Cochise, who was of a basically sympathetic and friendly nature, also sighed.

Jack glanced at him sourly. "Ain't there a couple o' flats to fix inside?"

"Surely are," Cochise agreed, bobbing his head on his awesome, horse-collar neck.

"Well, then," Jack said in some exasperation, "don't you think you should be lookin' after them?"

"Probably should," Cochise agreed amiably, still bobbing his head.

"So?"

"So?"

"So get to them! Now!"

"Oh, okay. Sure thing." Cochise smiled brightly and lumbered off.

Jack stood looking at the Kenworth, wiping

his hands slowly on a rag. "Parts come from Lincoln," he told Harold.

"Well, go ahead. I sure don't have much choice."

"Cash or check?"

"Check."

"Have to call your bank."

"City National. Des Moines."

"Cochise," Jack shouted toward the station. "Call Sandy and see how he's fixed for axles." He said to Harold, "The calls go on the bill."

Within the trailer, the cattle set to bawling. They bumped around against the walls.

"What about the cows?" Texaco Jack said.

"What about them?"

"I don't want them gettin' restless and breakin' up the garage. Or shittin' on my blacktop."

"They aren't goin' anywhere. And, hell, they'd have to shit sideways through the slats to hit your blacktop."

"Just so they don't." Jack turned away and headed for his office.

Hooves shifted within the trailer. There was a sudden liquid plosive sound, and a wad of steaming material shot out of the trailer and landed near Harold with a *plop!*, spattering his boots.

Harold looked down without expression. He shook his head. He wanted to cry.

Instead, he picked up an old sheet of newspaper from the ground and cleaned his boots off. Then he fished out the pouch of coins he'd taken from the cab of his truck and walked over to the pay phones on the side of the station. He dropped a dime in one and dialed O, gave the operator a Dallas number. She told him the charge for the first three minutes. He fed quarters into the slot. The phone went *bong, bong, bong.* The line was busy.

"Keep trying, operator. I'll wait for you to get back."

He hung up the receiver, stepped over to the second phone, put in a dime and dialed O.

"Hello, operator. I want to call Des Moines. Right. 515-255-3099."

He slipped the right amount of quarters into the phone.

The call was answered on the third ring.

"Hey, Petie? How ya doin', champ? Good. Is Mommy around? Good. . . . Hey, Joyce! How ya doin? Yeah. Union. Little trouble. Don't know yet. No, just a scratch. Really. No, don't come down. . . . Sure I'm sure."

The first phone rang. "Just a minute," he said to Joyce. He cradled the second phone in his arm and answered the first. "Hi, operator. Thanks. Just a minute."

He cradled the first phone and raised the second. "Hey, I love you. I miss you. I'm fine. I'm fine. Really. See you on Tuesday. Love to the boys." He hung up, a little homesick, missing Joyce and the boys, but bouyed by having talked with her.

He spoke into the first phone. "Hey, Connie. Yeah, Union. Little accident. Of course that's all. What else would I be doing here? . . . Well, all right then. How're the girls? . . ."

When he was done, he hung up, a little homesick, missing Connie and the girls, but bouyed by having talked with her.

CHAPTER 4

Harold was standing on the Kenworth's massive front bumper lovingly polishing the hood ornament—a chrome head and torso of a naked and winged woman, her back arched, hair flowing, proud breasts outthrust, and tiny little nipples erect.

Texaco Jack came out of the station and ambled over to him. "They gotta go to Omaha for parts," he said.

"How long?"

"Couple of days."

"Jesus, I got a delivery contract. Isn't there any other way?"

"Omaha," Jack repeated.

Harold sighed. "How 'bout a lift then?"

Jack looked doubtful.

"I'll pay for the gas," Harold said.

Jack nodded. "Cochise," he called.

In Cochise's Jeep, Harold settled down and lit a cigarette.

Cochise's CB picked up a young voice.

"Hey, Hustler."

"This is the Hustler. Go."

"Did you see Margie Frankel at the dance?"

"She's a total fox, a total fox," the Hustler said. "But she's sixteen and always on the rag."

"That's what I thought."

Cochise turned the set off and shook his head good-humoredly. "Those kids, boy, they're all over the air. And girls, that's all the one they call the Hustler ever talks about."

"Can't understand it," Harold said abstractedly. He was thinking about Joyce and Connie.

The Union High School gym had a gleaming polyurethaned floor and a high, girdered ceiling. Class was ending. Dean Lovejoy's voice echoed boomingly.

"All right! Everyone fall in! Ten-shun!"

Twenty-five ninth graders of varying angularity, height, and corpulence scrambled into a ragged line. They wore sneakers, blue shorts, and white T-shirts.

Dean tapped his foot impatiently while they tried to arrange themselves into some kind of order. He was thirty, crew-cutted, handsome in a blunt, square-jawed way, had a chunky, muscled body and hairy legs. He too wore sneakers and shorts, and a nylon jacket with Union High's emblem. A whistle hung from a cord around his neck. He carried a clipboard.

A spindly kid with glasses shifted uncomfortably in the line.

"Mr. Lovejoy," he said. "Can I go to the bathroom?"

"Should've thought about that before class, Connors."

Dean blew his whistle.

"All right, quiet down! Ten-shun! Dress right, dress! Let's go—shape it up there, shape it up! C'mon, Connors! What're you using for brains today! All right . . . at ease!"

Dean walked up and down the line, slapping his clipboard against his leg.

"I'm gonna run a uniform inspection now. When I pass I want you to pull out your supporter and snap it back. I wanna hear it snap, understand?"

He went to the head of the line and started down, scrutinizing each boy and waiting to hear the snap of his supporter before moving on.

He paused before Connors, stopped by a weak *phtt* instead of a snap.

"What is that, the elastic in your jockey shorts?"

"Yes, sir," Connors said miserably.

"Where's your supporter?"

"Uh, my mother's washing it."

The other boys in the line snickered, enjoying Connors' unhappiness.

"Gimme fifteen laps."

Connors started out around the edge of the gym.

Dean continued down the line, the snap of the jocks as pleasing as chamber music to a flutist.

Spider appeared in the doorway between the locker rooms and the gym. He leaned against the jamb, watching his older brother and the class.

Dean stopped before a tall, sinewy boy who stood easily and confidently in a pair of white sweat socks.

"Where're your shoes, Simon?"

"Forgot 'em," Simon said with an easy smile.

"You gonna remember 'em tomorrow?"

"Yeah."

"All right. The team needs you, boy. You want to be careful of gym demerits."

"Sure."

Connors passed on his third lap, already breathing hard, and looking as if he were in agony.

"Mr. Lovejoy," he called. "I really gotta go to the bathroom!"

Dean answered without looking at him. "Five extra laps, Connors. That makes twenty. You wanna try for five more?"

Connors jogged nearer to Spider, his face a contorted grimace.

Spider was overcome with compassion for the boy—he himself had been a spindly, awkward kid in high school, and it was clear that Dean had a special dislike for Connors.

"Hey, kid," he called in a loud whisper. "Go to the bathroom. I'm the coach's brother. I'll handle him for you."

Connors slowed, turned his head to look with fearful skepticism at Dean, then back to Spider.

"Go on," Spider said. "I'll take care of it."

Connors ran in place a moment, then relief flooded his face and he bolted for the locker room.

Dean caught movement from the corner of his eye and looked up, just as Connors disappeared from sight.

"Blaine," he said. "What did you just do?"

Spider waved. "Hey, Dean."

"What the hell did you just do?" Dean demanded.

"I just came by to say hello."

"You said something to that boy." Dean's face was turning crimson. "What did you tell him?"

The class was giggling.

Dean whirled on them. "All right! Everyone into the showers! Right now! Double-time! Let's move! Move! Move!"

The class broke ranks and started for the showers.

Dean came over to Spider. "What the fuck is this?"

"Hey, easy, Dean. . . ."

"You come in here, you deliberately disrupt my class—"

"Take it easy, I only wanted to—"

"Don't tell me to take it easy. This is my class, my gym, and I don't need you disrupting things. Now I want to know what the fuck you're trying to do here!"

"If you wouldn't be such a horse's ass and listen for one minute—"

"Don't push me."

"Well, you *are* acting like a horse's ass."

"You're pushing me—"

"I'm not pushing you."

Dean clenched a heavy hand into a fist. "I'll lay you right out on this floor. I mean it."

"I don't believe this," Spider said, raising his eyes to the ceiling, calling on God to witness the absurdity of it all.

"I swear! I'll lay you out!"

Spider stepped backward. His own hands started to curl up.

"Ain't never happened yet," he said coolly.

The doors on the other side of the gym swung open with a bang, and the ninth grade girls' class came jostling and shouting in. They were followed by Pam Armbruster, her lustrous chestnut hair pinned up, snug white shorts hugging her round bottom, a navy jersey fetchingly unable to conceal the bounce of her breasts. She carried a canvas bag filled with tennis balls.

Dean's features loosened. He put a big smile on his face and waved.

"Hi, Pam!"

Pam waved back. She paused a moment, eyes settling on Spider, then continued through the gym and outside to the tennis courts after her class.

Dean and Spider looked at each other awkwardly, tension mostly dissipated by the interruption.

Spider raised his hands. "Truce?"

"What do you want?" Dean asked.

Members of the school band began straggling into the gym.

"Let's go to your office," Spider said.

Dean's office was a glass-walled cubicle in one corner of the boys' locker room. There were shouts, belly-laughs, and horseplay, and the sound of banging locker doors. Dean sat behind his desk and Spider took a chair across from him.

Spider said, "I'd like some help with Pop, Dean. I can't seem to reach him anymore."

"You're the one who wanted to take care of everything."

"I'd like your help," Spider repeated.

"How?"

"Just make an effort to come around a little more. Spend some time with him. That's all. I can't handle it all, Dean. I really can't."

Dean looked away a moment. "I got no part, Blaine."

"What do you mean?"

"I got no part. Can we be honest about this?"

"Yeah. I want to be."

"Okay, then let's be honest. You were Mom's favorite. Donny is Dad's favorite. I got no part."

"That's not true."

"Roy don't count. He was always out fucking— broads, trees, squirrels, expired parking meters. I don't know."

"That's just not true."

"Will you agree with me on Donny?"

"Okay, maybe Donny. But that's it."

Dean laced his fingers together and looked at them. "And when Mom was upstairs dying those days . . . who did she call for? Did she call for me?"

"I told you what she said to me."

To the side of Dean, through the glass partition, Spider saw the athletic kid, Simon, and two others. They were giving Dean the finger. They were miming masturbation and convulsing in silent laughter.

Spider became angry on Dean's behalf, but he didn't say anything to his brother, to save him from the humiliation.

"I was waiting down there, praying and crying like the rest," Dean said. "But she didn't call me. She didn't tell me nothing."

"She only said one thing—'Don't let Ned's bowl go for more than two days.' That's all, Dean. I swear. There was nothing else in her mind."

Dean breathed deeply. "Let's drop it."

"Okay, but that's the truth."

"How is Ned the Dog?"

Spider smiled. "Smells like always. Shitty. You want him?"

"No. He's your dog."

"The hell he is." Spider waited a beat, then said, "Look, Dean, Pop's gonna be sixty-five next week. I want to do something special for him."

"What?"

"I don't know. Maybe a birthday party. Something like that."

"You mean just us?"

"Well, Roy's somewhere in Alaska and Donny's in the can. Who else?"

"Great party," Dean mumbled.

"If you want to invite someone, go ahead. We'll get a cake. Have some beers. He likes that kind of thing."

Dean didn't say anything.

"He's getting old, Dean. I didn't see it before, but now I do. You know, a little flaky around the edges."

"Fact is, he never cared for me much."

"Well, the way I see it—you're my brother. And that makes you his son. You know?"

Dean leaned back and stared at the ceiling. After a few moments, he said, "I'll give you a call."

Spider walked across the gym field toward the parking lot. He could see Ned waiting patiently in the Nomad, nose pressed through the space between the lowered window and the door frame.

"Blaine! Wait a minute!"

Pam was jogging from her class in his direction. He stopped. She caught up to him.

There was a nip in the air and she was chilled, despite the physical activity, and goose bumps prickled on her arms and legs. She looked terrific. Spider's heart rose up to his throat and lodged there.

They looked at each other in uneasy silence a moment, then Pam said, "How are you?"

"Okay. And you?"

"Fine. . . . How's your dad?"

"Fine."

"Good."

Her eyes looked deep into his, searching. He lowered his vision and examined his shoes.

"I—I still have some of your stuff," she said quietly. "You left a shirt."

Spider nodded. "Green? Yellow stripes?"

"Yes."

"I wondered where it went."

"And a walkie-talkie and a needle-nose pliers. Will you pick them up?"

"Okay. When?"

"The sooner the better, I think. This afternoon."

"Okay."

They stood a moment longer, awkwardly, since neither could think of anything more to say. Then, as if by agreement, they nodded shortly and each turned away, Spider toward the parking lot, and Pam back to her class.

Debbie Price lived in one of the Cosy Cove's nicer cabins (Magic Finger Mattresses & 3-Channel Television in Every Unit), which meant that the walls weren't as stained, the gas stove worked most of the time, and you could usually get hot water out of the hot-water tap.

There were three rooms in the cabin—a kitchen about the size of a double closet, a living room with furniture that wasn't too awfully old, and a big oversized bedroom. This last, considering it was where she spent most of her time, was the nicest part about it.

Debbie was thirty-eight but passed herself off as thirty-two and usually got away with it. She was plump, with generous nurturing breasts and round soft hips, a firm dense bottom that could really set the big queen-size bed in the bedroom—her own, what the management supplied just wouldn't do—to rocking when she threw herself into it. She had a round, nonjudgmental, sympathetic, and trust-inspiring face that was pretty in a home-body way. Her skin was her best single feature, smooth and clear as a fall morning.

Her CB set rested on a small dinette in the living room. She sat before it with a steaming cup of tea (twist of lemon, three sugars—her sweet tooth was implacable). She sipped, keyed the mike.

"Hey, all you lonesome cowboys with ears," she said cheerfully. "This here's Hot Coffee wishing you a doggone top o' the morning."

She sipped again, glanced out the window to the fine, crisp, sun-showered morning that had followed last night's storm.

"Mercy. We got one fine day here. Anyone wantin' to dunk their donuts in some hundred-mile perk-me-up, how about a taste o' some real down-home Hot Coffee, the way you like it? We're clear."

A jeep with a defective muffler came roaring

and coughing up to a stop before her cottage. Hot Coffee glanced out and saw a familiar figure jump from the Jeep and start toward her door.

She turned off her set, got up, and jerked the door open. "Harold! I didn't expect you till next week!"

CHAPTER 5

Hot Coffee turned back the bed. The sheets were fresh—crisply laundered. Harold, who had just finished fascinating her with the tale of his accident, sat down on the edge, pulled off his boots and let them fall to the floor, and stripped off his socks.

Hot Coffee lifted her sweater over her head. Her breasts were moderate, pleasing, round and wholesome. Like what you'd expect on a cheerleader. She loosened the waistband of her slacks and slid them down over her hips, balanced on one leg, then the other, to slide them off.

Harold slipped his shirt gingerly over his cast.

"When it starts to hurt," Hot Coffee said, "sometimes you can concentrate real hard on the pain and fool yourself into enjoying it. I do that at the dentist."

Harold stood to drop his own pants. "No, I'm

54

fine. I just thank my stars that fella showed up when he did."

He leered theatrically at the sexy little bikini briefs she was wearing.

Hot Coffee turned with feigned embarrassment to the side. She slid the briefs down coyly, maidenly modest, which was a kind of little joke they shared.

"How's Connie?" she asked.

"Fine."

"How'd that PTA meeting go?"

"What meeting?" Harold asked, dressed only in shirt and undershirt now.

"I don't know. Last time you mentioned something about a PTA meeting." Her briefs lay circled around one ankle. "Ta-ra!" She kicked her leg, launching the briefs toward Harold, who shot his arm up as they sailed overhead and caught them.

"I got the bouquet," he said.

"Then you're the lucky winner."

"Yeah, I remember the meeting now. Connie was really something. She gave that school board a good piece of her mind. It was about some smutty texts they wanted to bring into the classroom."

Harold shed his shirt and undershirt, got on the bed, and stretched out on his back with a contented sigh.

Hot Coffee got on, straddled his tummy. "How do you want it—half-and-half or straight up?"

"Uh. . . . Harold said, reflecting with pleasant anticipation. "Half-and-half."

Hot Coffee slid down. Harold looked idly up at the ceiling while she took him in. A slow happy smile began to spread across his face.

"So after Connie gets done giving them hell," he continued, "they banned the books and—oh yes, that's very nice—and they fired the teacher. I figure what the hell, the kids'll pick it up anyhow—um, yes—sooner or later. But Connie feels strong about it, so I say good for her."

Hot Coffee, of course, offered no further verbal comment.

In Hot Coffee's kitchen, a thoroughly enjoyable hour later, Harold took his first sip of the coffee she'd set before him.

"Mm-mmm!" he said. "I've been all over and nobody, but nobody makes it like you." He gave her a big wink.

She was wearing a bathrobe. Her hair was loose, pretty, and her face was soft and satisfied. She rolled her hips at him. "That's because I grind my own beans."

"Just *de*-licious," Harold said.

She looked at him over her shoulder. "It's part Colombian and part French Roast. That's why it's creamy, yet full-bodied."

"I just love that creamy full-bodied part. I can't tell you how much I love it."

"You don't have to, sugar. I noticed. I surely did." She poured a cup for herself and sat down across from him.

"Are things going any better for you?" he asked.

Her expression became serious. "It's just not good, Harold. Right now you're my only steady left."

"Can I help?"

"Thanks, but I don't see how. I just don't have the business anymore. First there was that bond issue and they moved the highway on me."

Harold nodded. "I remember that."

"Okay, things fell off a little, but a lot of the boys still came a bit out of their way. But now with that goddarned fifty-five speed limit, nobody has time for nothing. Those boys are working so hard to make their truck payments, they don't have time to catch their breath, much less stop here. Sometimes with the government doing these things to me, I wonder why I bother paying taxes." She stared morosely down at her cup.

"You don't pay taxes," Harold said.

She grew indignant. "I pay sales tax when I buy something, don't I?"

"Sure, but—"

"No buts. I pay taxes."

Harold put his hand over hers. "You shouldn't let it get you down so much."

"I don't see it growing any better," she said glumly. "I don't know what I'm going to do."

Harold scratched his head. His forehead creased in thought, then his face brightened. "I got an idea."

"What?"

"You know," he said with some excitement, "it's a funny country. Everything's mobile. I've been thinking a lot about it—you know, what it does to you. The good and the bad."

"And?"

Harold leaned back in his chair, pleased with himself. "When the founding fathers invented things," he said, in the tone of old Mr. Peabody, who was the teacher he remembered best from his school days, "I think they also invented roller skates. That's why you got a father there, a grandparent here, a child there all over the place." He checked Hot Coffee's face to see that she was following him. She was, as he had expected. She was a bright lady. Not as quick as he, perhaps, but pretty bright anyway. "It's like everybody's on wheels and nobody's slowing down. You see?"

"I never thought of it that way," Hot Coffee said, marveling at his insight.

"Do you have any appointments tomorrow morning?"

"No. Why?"

"I got an idea for you." Harold let her hang for a few moments, enjoying her suspense. It was kind of like flirting.

Spider pulled his Nomad around behind CB-er's Haven, which had the most complete stock of the couple of shops in town. And they handled a better grade of equipment too.

The Nazi—that's how he identified himself, which didn't make Spider any more fond of him than did the things he had to say—broke onto the air again.

"Hot damn!" said his raspy voice from the speaker. "This welfare sandwich is good and hot!" There were gross chewing sounds. "Now I know that some of you peapickers wanna use the channel." He paused to belch. "But the thing is, we know what I'm running here—and there ain't none of you that can compete with that kind o' power—so I guess it's all up to me. That's for peapickin' sure. But I'll tell you what. I gotta go to the little boy's room. So if you're good, I'll let you have it till I get back." He belched again and went off the air.

Spider shook his head. Some people, man.

He took the sets he'd repaired out of the trunk and carried them in to the stockroom. He gave them a final check-over by eye, then pulled each of the repair tags off along the perforated lines and walked into the front of the shop.

It was of modest size, but densely stocked. It was well ordered and spotless like the owner, Carter Purseworthy, who was tall, immaculately groomed, had capped teeth, and had attended the state university two years—a fact of which he was immensely proud, and which he reckoned made him one of the town's leading intellectuals.

Business was booming. Carter was just ringing up a sizeable sale, and there were half a dozen other customers in the shop, most looking serious and in a buying mood. In the few open spaces on the walls were hung signs that said things like, SAVE FLOORS, USE ASHTRAYS and PLEASE DON'T SMUDGE THE DISPLAY CASE. Carter was the kind of man who became hysterical over a lipstick smear on a drinking glass.

Carter bagged his customer's new equipment, slid it over to the outstretched hands, and said, "Congratulations. You bought a winner. It'll give you all the talk power you need."

"I hope so," the man said. "It's a real jungle out there. Do you listen much?"

"Not a chance," Carter said. "It'd drive me crazy."

When the man left, Spider motioned Carter aside. "Here are the repair slips," he said. "That Cobra Twenty-nine, the one that was driving everyone crazy, had a short in the jack. It's like new now."

"Good. We've got four more in the back. I wrote down the problems. And five installations to do tomorrow. Okay?"

"Yeah, I can handle it. You got a minute?"

Carter glanced around at his customers, none of whom seemed to require him immediately. "Yes, but only a minute."

Spider led him out the front door and onto the sidewalk. He pointed to a sign in the window. It was huge, a banner that spanned the entire width. It said: WE'VE GOT 'EM! 400-WATT LINEAR AMPS! NOT LEGAL FOR CB USE.

"What's that say to you?" Spider asked.

Carter shrugged. "Just what it says."

"Well, it says to me that they'll work nicely with CB equipment. And that's illegal."

Carter smiled. "It's only illegal to use them. It's not illegal to *sell* them."

Spider made a face. "Let's not play word games."

"Oh, lighten up. It makes the idiots happy. Who's it going to hurt?"

CHAPTER 6

THE NAZI CAME ON AGAIN AS SPIDER WAS DRIVING from CB-er's Haven over to Pam's house.

"You peapickers have a nice talk?" he asked. "'Scuse me while I take off my shirt. I don't wanna give you CB-ers bad habits, but of course if you peapickers don't like mine you can go back to Moscow or Africa or wherever you belong, that's for peapickin' sure."

Spider scowled at the set. He flicked it off.

Pam lived in a one-bedroom clapboard house, a little crackerbox of an affair, but she kept it neat and in good condition, and she'd planted flowerbeds and shrubbery around it. He parked at the curb and walked up to the front door. The crocuses were just beginning to erupt from beneath the dark mold of the topsoil in the flower beds. He had helped her put in some of the flowers last year. Those had been fun afternoons, kneeling in blue jeans in the dirt and digging in bulbs with hand trowels. He felt melancholy and sad.

He knocked.

"Come on in, Blaine," she called from within. The door was unlocked.

Pam came out of the kitchen, drying her hands on a dish towel. She wore jeans and a chambray shirt a little too big for her. The tails were knotted over her midriff.

Spider looked around the living room. There were a couple of new pieces—a lamp, a magazine stand, one or two other odds and ends—and everything was spotless.

"The place looks good," he said.

"Thank you. There was a shopping bag around here somewhere." She pursed her lips, put a finger to them, and cast her eyes about.

"Hey," Spider said. "I heard you went to Omaha for the Olympic tryouts."

"Yes. I think maybe I left it in the kitchen. Excuse me." She exited and returned a moment later with the bag. "Yup. Your things are in here."

"How'd you do there?" he asked.

"Okay. What do you want to do with the CB?"

"Did you place?"

"No."

"Lousy judging, huh?"

"What about the CB?"

"Do you use it?"

"A little."

Spider shrugged. "I don't need it. Use it as long as you want."

"What about this?" She held up a small velvet box with an engagement ring inside.

"That's yours."

"Not anymore."

"It's yours," Spider insisted.

"Blaine—"

He ran his finger over the top of a table, then examined it. No dust had come off on his skin. "Why all the spring cleaning? Are you seeing someone else?"

Pam looked away.

"That's it, isn't it?" he said. "You're seeing someone else."

"It's been three months, Blaine," she said quietly.

"Oh. Well, that's fine. I'm glad for you." He bounced up on his toes, looked around the room beaming. "Who is he?"

"I'd rather not talk about it."

"Someone I know?"

"I said I don't want to talk about it."

Spider nodded. "Okay. How tall is he, then? Taller than me?"

"I don't see what that—"

"You can tell me that much, can't you? Come on, just that. Is he taller than me?"

Pam sighed. "All right, Blaine. No, he's not taller than you."

"About the same?"

"Blaine!"

"Come on, that's not much. The same?"

"No," Pam said with resignation.

"Shorter?"

"Yes, he's a little shorter than you, okay? Now will you please—"

"What kind of car does he drive?"

"Blaine, I don't understand—"

"I'm asking what kind of car he drives! Am I asking too much?"

"Yes, you are—I don't know what kind of car—"

"Is it big?"

"No."

"Small?"

"Yes, it's small."

"American?"

"No."

"Blue? Green? Pink?"

"White. It's white."

Spider snorted. "Now we're getting somewhere. He's short and drives a small foreign car." The corners of his mouth curled down. "Sounds like a real twerp!"

"He's not."

Spider opened the bag and rummaged through it, probing the bottom with his hand. "Are my pliers in here?"

"He's not a twerp, Blaine," Pam said seriously.

Spider's shoulders sagged. He looked suddenly very tired.

"Are you okay?" Pam asked.

"Frankly, Pam, at this moment I'm concerned about your future. Very concerned."

"I appreciate that," she said in a tone that clearly indicated the opposite.

"Well," Spider said. "Well. . . ." He turned to leave, stopped, turned back. "If you need me for anything. . . ."

Pam opened the door. "Right. Thank you."

Reluctantly Spider stepped outside to the stoop.

"Bye," he said.

"Bye."

Pam closed the door. She leaned against it, hugged herself.

There was a knock.

She slid back the cover from the small viewing grate in the center. Spider was bent over, face close to the grate, staring in.

"You sure you don't need the needle-nose for anything?"

"I'm sure. Thank you."

"Right."

Pam slid the cover back and turned away. Spider knocked again. With a little groan she went back and opened the grate again.

"But I still love you," Spider said.

She closed the grate.

Spider was out driving—not going anywhere, just driving. He did that when he was unhappy or had something on his mind. The droning engine and monotonous hiss of the tires against the pavement helped to soothe and relax him. On such drives he kept his CB off. He did not want the outside world to intrude upon his reverie.

Spider had managed to shrink his consciousness down to nothing, driving by instinct and pure reflex, and felt the sourness beginning to drain from his spirit.

This happy state was suddenly and jarringly interrupted by a tremendous roar and a great whoosh of air that tugged at the Nomad and skittered it a few inches to the side.

Spider snapped totally alert and fought the wheel.

A small single-engine two-seater plane came swooping at a diagonal across the highway less than a dozen feet above the ground and only a few yards in front of him.

"Holy Christ!" Spider swerved violently. The Nomad went skidding sideways down the road.

The plane shot over the macadam and clipped a telephone pole with its wing. The wing sheared off and the plane somersaulted into a thicket of brush and burst into flame.

Spider brought his car under control. His momentum had carried him a hundred yards past the crash site. He threw the Nomad into reverse and stomped on the accelerator, burning rubber all the way back. He grabbed his mike.

"Breaker! Breaker! Breaker! I need a React Monitor! A React Monitor! Emergency! Ten-thirty-three. Ten-thirty-eight!"

"Do you know Leslie Cinworth?" the Hustler's voice asked.

"No," another boy answered. "Do you know Sandy Lankerman?"

"Break, Break!" Spider screamed. "Clear the channel! React Monitor!"

He spun the Nomad around and gunned it across the field, bouncing crazily toward the burning plane.

"She goes to Hadley."

"Blonde hair? Big tits?" the Hustler asked.

"No, that's Sandy Stigwood."

Spider slammed the Nomad to a halt. "Break! Break!"

"I think someone's trying to step on us," the boy said.

"Some people are so rude," the Hustler said.

Spider threw down the mike in disgust, grabbed the fire extinguisher clipped beneath the dash, and leaped from the car. He circled the burning wreckage spraying foam, pushing into the dense black smoke to look for survivors. He caught sight of the pilot, a middle-aged man with a badly lacerated face, fumbling ineffectually to free himself from his seat belt. Spider smashed the glass of the door with his fire extinguisher, reached in, released the seat belt and jerked open the door. He pulled the man out and dragged him away from the flaming plane to safety. Then he ran back to the Nomad, dove onto the front seat and grabbed the mike again.

"Clear the channel! Immediately! Emergency!"

"He's back," the boy said.

"Hey, dude," the Hustler said peevishly. "We don't know who you are, but there are other people in this world besides you."

Outside, three or four cars had drawn up beside the Nomad. Their occupants were out and they clustered uncertainly some thirty yards from the burning plane, shielding their faces from the intense heat and staring with open mouths.

A man in a Norwegian ski sweater, whose wife looked as if she were going to be ill, turned to a college kid in wire-framed glasses and a beard.

"Did anyone go for help," the man in the ski sweater said. "You think one of us should get to a phone?"

The younger man shook his head. "No, it's okay. The guy back there in the Nomad is on his CB."

Much later, a little past midnight, Spider was sitting at a round, rough-cut, varnished pine table in the Red Herring Bar & Grill. Cochise was there with him, and Texaco Jack, and a couple of other guys who sometimes hung around—okay people who shared an interest in good cars and the useful and fun possibilities of CB. There were half a dozen empty and half-empty beer pitchers before them.

Spider was quiet and moody, had an angry cast to his mouth.

A guy named Cal, who had a droopy Pancho Villa moustache, said, "Look at it this way. You saved Fenton's neck. It all worked out in the end."

Texaco Jack scratched his big gut lazily. "If you let them get on your case, Spider, you won't have any fun with your radio."

Cochise, who was seated across from Spider, nodded without looking up from the elaborate airplane he was sketching on a pad.

Ray, an old high school teammate of Spider's said, "There's nothing you can do about it. Big D tried for a while. Busted a few antennas. Scared some kids. But he finally gave it up. Moved to Channel Three. He says he's got a lot of friends on Three now."

Ray's brother, Tony, said, "So many turkeys out there, all we can do is go to sideband. But they'll all get there eventually."

"Ten's the real idiot channel," Cal said.

Tony shook his head. "They're all idiot channels."

"What about that Triple-X, the bucketmouth who reads porno over Twenty?" Texaco Jack said. "With all the kids out there and everything. I tried sending some carriers his way, but he must be pumping some bodacious power. I couldn't touch him."

Les, who helped out at Texaco Jack's station on weekends, and who subscribed to and passionately read every skin and sex magazine he could find, perked up at the mention of Triple-X and broke his characteristic silence to add, "I understand there's some chick called Electra who's been strokin' off the high schoolers right over the air. I haven't been able to tune her in myself, but I heard a lot of talk. Strokes 'em right off, she does."

"*Shit*," said Tony.

Texaco Jack smirked. "Probably some big ugly broad with hair comin' out of her ears who can't get it anywhere else."

"Nothing you can do about it," Ray said. "Tony tried going to the FCC. That's a joke."

"Yeah. I wrote to them," Tony said. "The truth is, all you can do is get the offender's call letters, but nobody bothers with a license anymore. More turkeys in the FCC than on the band, that's for sure."

Cal shook his head. "It's the electronics lobby that calls the shots. They own the FCC. The FCC ain't shit. It's the electronics lobby—talk about power and greed."

"You know who really done this to us?" Texaco Jack demanded.

"Who?" said Cal.

"Who *really* done it?" Texas Jack paused and looked around meaningfully. He lowered his voice, as if there might be dangerous eavesdroppers. "Richard Nixon."

There was some headshaking, some thoughtful murmuring.

"Well, *I* didn't vote for him," Tony said indignantly.

"Me neither," chorused Ray.

Les, recalling the former President's hostile

stance against pornography, said, "*I* sure didn't."

Spider pushed his chair back and stood up. "I'll see you guys later," he said, tossing a couple of dollars onto the table.

"Where you going?" Texas Jack asked.

"To clean up the band."

"And how're you gonna do that?" Ray asked.

Spider smiled unpleasantly. "Kick ass." He turned and stalked out.

Everyone at the table looked after him.

"He'll do it too," Texas Jack said thoughtfully.

"When it comes to CB-ing," Ray said, "Spider's always been a real purist."

"Ain't no place for them today," Tony said.

"For who?"

"What you said."

"Purists?"

"Yeah."

"He'll do it too," Texas Jack repeated.

CHAPTER 7

HIS ANGER WAS PUFFED UP A BIT BY THE BEER
he'd drunk, but there was nothing false about it.
It was a hard little ball in the pit of his stomach.
It made a muscle in his cheek tic. It drew down
the corners of his mouth.

Spider's Nomad was pulled up beside his workshop. He had a trouble light running on a long
cord out through the door and hanging on a nail
on the wall. There was a burlap sack on the Nomad's hood and on top of it his tools were spread
out. He was mounting a signal-seeking loop antenna on the roof of his car. He tightened down
the nut and wiggled the antenna to test that it
was secure.

Then he opened the Nomad's door and got in.
He ran the coaxial cable from the antenna across
the upholstery of the roof, fixing it with strapping
tape, then forward above the door line, down

alongside the windshield, and across the dash. He hooked it up to his CB unit. He wired an unused circuit to power a flexible map light he'd screwed onto the dash, then hung a clipboard next to the lamp. He clipped a map of the Union city streets and the immediate outlying area to the board, and hung a pencil on a string next to it.

He went into the house, where his father was asleep and Ned was curled up on an old blanket next to the stove, and rummaged through a downstairs closet until he found an old baseball bat. He went back out and, with some affectionate care, like a cop gently shifting his gun in its holster, positioned the bat so that it was propped up against the passenger side, its butt in easy reach.

Pam's convertible appeared as he was taking down the trouble light. She pulled to a stop beside the Nomad and got out.

"Blaine?"

Surprised and pleased to see her, Blaine set down the trouble light and said, "Hey, Pam! What's up?"

She took her CB radio from her car. "Something's wrong with this thing. I keep losing my modulation."

Spider snorted when he took it, irritated that that was what had brought her here.

"I thought you didn't use it." He picked up a screwdriver and opened the radio.

"What are you doing with that antenna?" Pam asked.

"Ever hear of the Hustler? Or Triple X?"

"No."

Spider probed into the radio. "Or if you don't like them, we also got a phony priest selling Jesus over Seven, a Nazi keeping Four pure Aryan, and some gal called Electra who thinks she's the stroke-off queen of seventeen. . . ." He made an adjustment, screwed the chasis back on, and returned the radio to her. "Here. All fixed. Electra. Huh! Probably some big ugly broad with hair comin' out of her ears who can't get it anywhere else."

Unconsciously, Pam pulled at her ear. "I wouldn't doubt that."

"So long," Spider said, gathering up the trouble light and going into the workshop. He paused to warm his hands over the wood stove. Pam followed him. He ignored her and went to work on a line of amplifiers, wiring them together.

After several awkward moments of silence, Pam said, "Well . . . I hope you find who you're looking for." She turned abruptly on her heel and left.

Spider looked at the door several moments after she'd gone. "Damn!" he said. "Damn!" And then he went back to work on the amplifiers.

Linked, he tested them. The meters showed a bad connection somewhere. He traced it down in a few minutes, tested again, and this time it looked good. He flipped a switch—the instruments buzzed almost inaudibly and red indicator lights sprang on.

He picked up a mike.

"This is KKT6757, the Spider, speaking. Attention to all CB operators. I'm no longer running barefoot. Fact is, I got enough juice here to open up a radio station. So listen good. . . ."

His words went out across the city, and well into the rural areas beyond it. They were heard by night attendants in gas stations, by lonesome truckers barreling on through the night to desti-

nations far away, by a bored waitress in a road-
side cafe, by a bunch of kids out skylarking in a
painted van, by sleepless businessmen fiddling
with their base stations, by a simmering house-
wife whose husband should have been home
hours ago. . . .

"From now on," Spider said, "all CB operation
is to conform with Part Ninety-five of the FCC
Rules and Regulations."

He paused a beat, then his voice hardened.

"That means no idle chitchat, no profanity.
That means no deceptive transmissions, no operation without a license."

He paused again, to let his words sink in. Then
he said, "All violators will be dealt with severely.
I repeat: All violators will be dealt with severely.
This message will be repeated on each channel
daily."

So much for Channel One. He moved the selector to Channel Two and began again.

"This is KKT6757, the Spider, speaking. Attention all CB operators. . . ."

The sun was bright, and an ambitious wind
flapped the multicolored plastic pennants that
hung from high wires surrounding the Union Rec-
reational Vehicle Center.

Hot Coffee and Harold stood in the open lot
gazing at a long, sleek, chrome-trimmed Winnebago. A salesman stood discreetly a little to the
side, pretending that he was not trying to over-
hear them.

"It's very handsome," Hot Coffee said. "I can't
deny that."

"I see a lot of these on the road," Harold said.
"The owners I've talked to seem pretty enthusias-

tic. Go ahead, ask the gentleman any questions you want."

The salesman joined them quickly. "That's what I'm here for."

"Can I go inside?"

"Please do." The salesman opened the door for her.

The driver's area was carpeted and paneled, roomy, the windshield and side windows great open expanses of glass, the two swivel-mounted captain's chairs well cushioned and finished in imitation leather.

Immediately behind was the dining area, further back, bedroom and living room. There was an abundance of cabinets and storage trunks, pleasing little gadgets, paneling, merry curtains —so much that Hot Coffee couldn't suppress a gasp of surprised pleasure, which made the salesman beam.

"This model sleeps three standard," he said. "We also offer a five or seven option."

"Golly," Hot Coffee said. "That's plenty. I've never even done three."

Harold gave her a small jab in the ribs.

"This here's your kitchen," the salesman said, leading her back into the vehicle.

"Nice. What's this?" She rapped the wood-grained tabletop.

"Formica."

"Nice."

"Let me ask you something," the salesman said. "You'd never hoist your motor home several feet in the air and deliberately drop it, would you?"

"It would never occur to me," Hot Coffee admitted.

The salesman clapped his hands together.

"Well, sir—or, ma'm—that's exactly what Winnebago did to prove their structural integrity. It's called Thermosteel construction."

"Nice," Hot Coffee said.

"Now these divider curtains here push back to open up large living and entertaining areas. Like this. And closed—like this—they provide sleeping and dressing privacy."

"Nice, nice, nice," Hot Coffee said.

The salesman led her further back and opened a door. "This is your combination shower/tub."

"Nice," Hot Coffee said. "Are there any other fixtures available here?"

"What would you like?"

"Well. . . ." Hot Coffee went girlishly shy. "I've always sort of wanted a . . . bidet."

"A bidet?"

"It's French. . . ."

"Well, I'll certainly check the accessory catalog," the salesman said heartily. "What did you call it again?"

"A bidet."

"Yes, of course."

They left the vehicle. The salesman wanted them to come into the office while he did some figuring. Hot Coffee declined.

"Really, we're just looking."

"You might as well have all the facts."

"Thank you, but I think we'd rather talk about it a bit first."

"Tell you what, why don't you have a little conference here, and I'll run in and check on that, uh, that bidet thing for you." He was off at a sprint before Hot Coffee could reply.

"Well, what do you think?" Harold asked.

"It's lovely and everything, but who can afford it?"

"Forget about the money for a minute," Harold pressed. "Do you like it?"

"Sure. Who wouldn't?"

"Okay. That's what's important. Now, tell me, you pay rent at the Cozy Cove, don't you?"

"They don't give me the place free because they think I'm a deserving child."

"Then let's do this. I'll put enough down to make the monthly payments the same as your rent. All you have to do is meet the payments. Okay?"

"Harold," she said, with appreciation and embarrassment, "I can't let you do that."

"Hey, I want to."

"But that's a lot of money," she protested.

"Look, the other night that guy saved my life. I'm just glad to be here. The money's not important. I'm happy to be able to do it for you."

The salesman, who didn't look quite as jovial as he had before, when things were looking more promising, came jogging back to them.

"Sir," Harold said, before the man could speak. "Why don't we move to the office? The lady doesn't like this color one bit."

The salesman's face lit up anew. "Certainly! We have several different colors, and combinations of colors, and we've got painters if you don't like the colors we have, and—"

"The office?" Harold repeated.

"Of course, of course!" He took both their arms. "Right this way!"

Hot Coffee looked across the salesman to Harold. "You really are something," she said. "How am I ever going to repay you?"

Harold gave her a broad wink. "We'll think of something, babe. We'll think of something."

Spider was bent over a dismantled toaster in his workshop, a screwdriver in hand.

The CB behind him broke its silence.

"Hey, Hustler. You out there?"

"Yeah. I'm here. Who's that?"

"The Red Dragon. Kenny said you wanted to talk to me."

"Yeah, that's right."

"Then go, Hustler."

"Who were you with at the game—Wendy K.?"

"Yeah."

"Did she go down on you?"

"Yeah . . . well . . . you know. . . ."

"I hear she gives good head."

"How would you know that?"

"Hey, dude, you're talkin' to the Hustler. How ya think I'd know?"

Spider flung down the screwdriver and grabbed the mike. "Breaker. Breaker. This is KKT6757, the Spider, speaking. From now on all CB operation is to conform with. . . ."

Pam's office, she being only an assistant P.E. instructor, was smaller than Miss Hadey's (who was the department head), and located on the other side of the girls' locker room, near the bin where the soiled towels were thrown after the showers.

Pam was at her desk looking over the medical report of a girl who'd broken her nose on a trampoline the week before. It was nothing serious, but regulations required she submit a report to the Board of Ed by Friday.

There was a knock on the door.

Pam looked up to see one of her third-year students, Karen Dugan, a cute, slightly plump little girl with wide blue eyes. Karen was normally bouncy and energetic, a high-spirited jokester. but now her shoulders were slumped and she wore a hangdog expression. Pam waved her in.

"Can I talk to you a minute, Miss Armbruster," the girl said unhappily.

"Sure. Close the door and take a seat."

Karen sat, clasped her hands together in her lap, and stared at them. Her eyes glistened. "I think," she said after a few moments, "that Richie and I are breaking up."

Pam leaned back. "Why?"

"He . . . he wants to do things that I just don't want to do. He's been weird lately."

"Sexual things?"

Karen nodded, coloring. "And I just don't feel I'm ready for that."

"Did you tell him?"

"Yeah," Karen said miserably. "But it doesn't matter what I say or think. That's what I want to ask you. I read that women . . . you know, reach their . . . peak . . . at thirty, while men get theirs at seventeen. Is that true?"

Pam toyed thoughtfully with a pencil. "I've read that, Karen. But there are other factors to consider. You can't make a blanket generalization."

"Well, Richie's going to be seventeen in May. And I think he's peaking on me."

"What does he say about it?"

"He says abstinence poisons his system. That's why he's breaking out."

Pam smiled gently. "That's a new one. Tell him he should try washing his face."

Despite herself, Karen smiled too. Then she went serious again. "What should I do? He's really been weird lately."

"Certainly nothing you don't feel right about. I'm sure if he tries hard enough, the old Warlock can find other solutions to his cosmetic problems. I'm *quite* sure he can." Pam smiled again, enigmatically this time.

In the gym, Miss Hadey was inspecting her class. She was a stubby, pillar-bodied, muscular woman who wore glasses whose upper frames winged out in points that were sharp as a stiletto.

"Co-ed volleyball today, girls," she announced in a rough voice. "As soon as Coach Lovejoy can get his would-be he-men out of the locker room. I trust we all have our hair in place?"

She walked down the line, snapping her fingers with every other step, as if she longed for a riding crop. She stopped in front of Sandra Stahl.

Sandra was slight, almost skinny, with reddish hair and freckles. She frequently wore the expression of a small, startled animal. The girl seemed to shrink inward under Miss Hadey's gaze.

"Well, well, what do we have here?" Miss Hadey said with artificial sweetness.

She reached out delicately, pinched her thumb and forefinger on a tail of toilet paper peeping out from the top of Sandra's gym top, then pulled, unraveling a wad that Sandra had stuffed into her brassiere.

"Really, Sandra," she boomed, "I don't see how this will impress the boys one bit."

Sandra cried out. Her face turned crimson.

Tears flooded to her eyes. She clasped her hands to her face, whirled, and stumbled blindly out of line toward the locker room.

Miss Hadey called after her. "Now, now, we can't be *that* sensitive. Let's wash our face and return to class."

Pam had Karen laughing. The girl was relieved, self-assured again, and her buoyant spirits had returned.

They were interrupted by a crashing locker door. They both turned to look out the window.

Sandra Stahl came rushing by, her cheeks awash in tears, her mouth a grimace of humiliated torment.

Pam got up quickly. She patted Karen on the shoulder. "Excuse me, Karen. I think we have a casualty here. Come and see me if you have any more trouble with Richie, okay?"

Karen nodded. Pam hurried out to find Sandra.

The faculty lounge was on the second floor, spacious and well lighted by big windows, but a drab green color and appointed with uninspired and not very comfortable vinyl-covered couches and plastic chairs.

Pam had just dropped a quarter into the coffee machine when Miss Hadey swaggered over to her. They were alone in the lounge.

"I see that you and Dean Lovejoy are getting to be good friends," Miss Hadey said.

Pam made a noncommittal sound and watched the coffee fill the paper cup.

"I just want to remind you," Miss Hadey continued, "that there are certain appearances that must be maintained here." She arched a bushy eyebrow. "Need I say more?"

Pam turned slowly. "Are you talking to me?"

"Miss Armbruster, there were many applicants for your position, all highly qualified. We chose you because since you are a former student here, we thought you'd know the rules and play by them."

"Michelle," Pam said with a warm smile, "I have only two things to say to you. One—that was a shitty, unnecessary thing you did to Sandra Stahl today. And two—I know you get your jollies keeping the girls waiting for towels so you can check out their young butts."

Miss Hadey's nostrils flared. "I'll pretend I didn't hear that, Armbruster."

Pam pinched the older woman's cheek. "And I'll pretend you don't do that."

CHAPTER 8

PAM WAS IN BED WITH DEAN, RESTING. SHE SAID, "Maybe I'll go to Baltimore."

She had spoken before, offhandedly, of getting out of Union in the next year or so. She'd first raised the possibility just after she'd broken up with Spider, when she and Dean were only casual acquaintances.

"Baltimore?" Dean said with a chuckle, as if it were Anchorage or Mindanao.

"Don't ask me why. It just sounds right. I mean, who wants to go Tul-sa?"

"Not me," Dean said.

"Or Mi-am-i."

"Not me again."

"But Baltimore. . . ."

"Tul-sa. Mi-am-i. Bal-ti-more. It's all the same."

"I've been in one place too long. It's starting to do strange things to my head."

"How strange?" he said.

"Strange enough," Pam said, and did not elaborate. "Remember when you were about fourteen and you'd go back to visit your grade school? You'd be struck by two things more than anything else: first, the water fountains were lower than you remembered and, second, most of your teachers were still doing exactly the same things they were when you left. And you'd think the fountains were so cute and the teachers so pathetic. . . ."

"I never really thought about it that way, but, yeah, you're right."

"I don't want to be one of those fountains."

"You will never be a water fountain," he assured her.

"That's right. I won't allow it to happen."

"Are you serious about all this—about Baltimore?"

Pam shrugged, as if to say she didn't really know. She kissed Dean.

Dean said, "Maybe I'll go with you."

"Maybe you will." After a moment she said, "When?"

Dean thought.

"How 'bout Friday?" Pam said.

Dean furrowed his brow in deeper concentration.

"Okay," Pam said agreeably, "then how about Saturday?"

Dean shook his head. "It'll have to be after track. I've got track this spring."

The late afternoon sun slanted into Cochise's

room in knife-edged shafts. Motes of dust swam in the shafts.

Most of the wall space was covered with blueprints of complicated model airplanes, and there were three bookshelves crammed with texts on aviation design and aerodynamics.

Cochise was bent over his desk—an old door on sawhorses—like a great bear stooping to peer at something quizzical. Carefully he squeezed glue out of a tube that was absurdly small in the grip of the stuffed sausages of his fingers, threading it onto a balsa wood tail assembly. He positioned the rear of the fuselage of his big model into the open jaws of a gluing clamp, then pressed the tail assembly to it. Face screwed up in concentration, he turned the handle of the clamp with his other hand, bringing it into delicate contact.

His door opened. Spider stuck his head in. "Hey, Cochise. Ready to roll?"

"Just a minute."

The tail and fuselage were pressed together, but there was just the tiniest bit of play left. He turned the clamp handle another slow half revolution.

There was a sharp *crack*. The tail assembly split in two.

"Shoot!"

Spider laid a hand on his shoulder. "The Wright brothers had their problems too."

"I guess," Cochise said glumly. He pursed his lips. "Well, hell. What the hell. I got all morning tomorrow free."

They went down the worn, clean carpeting on the stairs and into the kitchen where Cochise paused to dump half a dozen doughnuts from the bread drawer into a paper bag.

His mother, a pretty, nice woman, the kind pictured on cake-mix boxes, was sweeping off the back porch when they emerged.

"Don't wait dinner, Ma," Cochise said. "I'll grab somethin' out. But you can put what's left into the oven for me when I get home."

"Have a good time, boys." They were part way across the yard when she said, "Oh, Blaine."

Spider turned back. Cochise went on to the Nomad.

"Yes?"

She brushed uncomfortably at her gray hair, her face soft but urgent. "My husband and I . . . we want to thank you for including Cochise . . . for helping him get the job at the gas station. You've always . . . been good to him . . . just including him. . . ." She faltered, unable to find satisfactory words.

"He's my friend," Spider said, and meant it.

"Never mind. You're a good boy." She dug into the pocket of her apron and extracted two wrinkled dollar bills. She held them out to Spider. "You take this now and—"

Spider stepped back and shook his head. "I can't."

Her eyes moistened. "Please."

"I can't. He's my friend."

She took his hand in both of hers and forced the money into his palm. "It's not much, I know. But it'll get you two a nice hamburger someplace."

"But—"

"Go on, now. Get." She took up her broom again and began sweeping energetically. "Get, I said."

Spider nodded, turned toward the Nomad.

The woman stopped sweeping and watched him go. "Thank you," she said quietly. "Thank you."

Cochise was bulked in the passenger seat, the seat belts unused. There wasn't a belt he'd ever seen that could get around him. Ned was in the back seat, panting in happiness, which made the car a rolling gas chamber.

Spider pulled out of the driveway. The car tilted sharply toward the passenger side. Spider eased over to the curb.

"Uh, Cochise, I think we're listing a little. How 'bout if you sit in the back. Uh, kind of in the middle—my springs are just about shot."

"Sure," Cochise said happily. He climbed in the back, trading places with Ned, who—suddenly confronted with the wide vistas presented by the windshield—decided, for some reason buried deep in his aging canine mind, to bark for several moments.

"Quiet, Ned," Spider said.

"Rooooff," Ned said, by way of coda.

Spider pulled away again.

"That's fine. Thanks, good buddy."

"No sweat."

They drove aimlessly for the better part of an hour, with Spider shifting the channel selector on his CB every few minutes.

They were passing the shopping plaza when he picked up a droning youthful voice:

"Fuck youuuu. . . . Fuck youuuu. . . . Fuck youuuu. . . ."

"Sweet, very sweet," Spider said in disgust.

"That sounds like the Hustler," Cochise said.

Spider bobbed his head in agreement. He turned the coaxial cable by hand, which shifted the loop antenna on the roof around. He kept an eye on the CB meter.

Cochise was leaning forward, watching closely. "Twenty degrees north," he said.

Spider glanced at the map. "We'll make a right at the next intersection. We're close."

"Fuck youuuu. . . ." crooned the Hustler.

Spider cruised down a side street of small ranch houses and bungalows.

"Ten degrees east," Cochise said.

"I think we passed it. Might be that blue house back there."

"Fuck youuu. . . ."

"Thirty degrees east," said Cochise.

"It is the blue one."

Spider glanced in the rearview mirror. He braked, put the car in reverse, and backed up, parked in front of a ranch house with blue aluminum siding, with two lamp posts flanking the walk. He picked up the baseball bat and got out of the car.

"Hit the horn if anyone shows," he said.

He went up to the door and knocked. After several moments there was the sound of a lock being turned, then the door was cracked some, and a peevish fourteen-year-old looked out. Spider recognized him from the school. He was that kid Connors, over whom he'd gotten into the argument with Dean in the gym. Connors was wearing a T-shirt. He'd stenciled "The Hustler" onto it. Spider looked down to the name, then back up at the kid's face, and smiled widely.

"What do you want?" the Hustler demanded.

"Is your mother or father home?"

"No."

"Good."

Spider kicked open the door and brushed past the kid.

"Haven't I seen you someplace before?" he said.

"Hey, you can't come in here!" the Hustler said angrily.

"You were in my brother's class."

"What class? What the hell are you talking about?"

"Where's the radio, Hustler?"

The Hustler's eyes narrowed. "What radio?"

"The CB. Where is it?"

"I don't have any radio. I don't know what you're talking about."

"Probably your room. Right?"

Spider turned toward the hallway.

"Hey, you get out of here!" the Hustler yelled. "Help! Police!"

Spider went down the hall opening doors and peering in. The last one on the right was hung with aluminum mobiles and Day-Glo posters, a couple of Playboy centerfolds. A CB transceiver stood on a small desk, over which hung a pennant from Union High.

"Nice rig," Spider said to the Hustler, who ran in after him. "You got a license?"

"Yeah," the kid snapped. "Now get the hell out of here. Police! Police!"

"Let's see it," Spider said.

"I don't have to show it to you."

"That's because you don't have one, right?"

"I don't care what you think."

"That's good, then you won't get upset." Spider began disconnecting wires from the set.

"Hey!" the kid yelled. "Cut it out! Police!"

He ran forward and jumped on Spider's back,

pummeled Spider about the head with his fists. Spider flipped him off easily, onto his bed, where he landed with a grunt.

"You've been using this set illegally," Spider said calmly. "No license. Lots of fuck-yous."

"I don't care what you think," the kid repeated in stupid belligerance. "You can't hurt me."

"I don't want to hurt you." Spider raised the bat over his head. "But I *am* taking you off the air."

He brought the bat down with all his strength. The unit's cabinet split open and circuit boards cracked into pieces.

The kid howled.

Spider cast a professional eye at the set—it was damaged beyond repair.

"All finished," he said.

He went out.

The kid followed him down the hall. "Go ahead! I don't care! My father'll buy me another one! Then he'll get you!"

As Spider stepped out of the house, the No-mad's horn blew. A woman in a station wagon filled with grocery bags had pulled into the drive and was getting out of the car.

The Hustler came out behind Spider, screaming and crying. He jumped up and down shrieking inarticulately and pointing at Spider.

The woman rushed to him and wrapped him protectively in her arms. "What is this? What's going on?"

"Mommy," the Hustler sobbed. "He broke into the house and smashed my radio!"

The woman's eyes widened. "He did what?"

"He broke my radio! My CB!"

The woman turned to Spider, locked her eyes

with his. "Thank God. I've been wanting to do that for months!"

Spider had been holding his breath. Now he exhaled with a loud sigh. He made a little bow to the woman.

"May I help you with your groceries?" he asked.

"Thank you."

"He broke my radio!" the Hustler screamed.

"Jamie," the woman said firmly, "get in the house and quit crying or I'll kick your butt in!"

CHAPTER 9

LIKE A SLOW PREDATOR, THE NOMAD ROLLED smoothly up and down a series of crescent and winding streets.

The elderly woman's voice rambled on happily from the CB: "In the spring, Tom took me to Milwaukee for my twenty-third birthday. Of course, we couldn't afford a car in those days, but the trains were real nice. Even the bathrooms. Well, Shirley was having her second child and we visited . . ."

"The old broad's been on forty-five minutes straight," Spider said.

"Thirty degrees south," said Cochise.

Oblivious, the voice continued. "Marnie was such a lovely baby, you could see the whole world in her eyes. . . ."

They found it, a neat little wooden house whose curtains were tied with a bow, potted geraniums in the window.

Spider got out of the Nomad and walked up to the door and knocked.

He was answered by a gray-haired woman in a wheelchair. She had bright spots of color on her cheeks and wore wire-rimmed glasses.

"Yes?" she said brightly.

Spider felt awkward. She looked like such a friendly, grandmotherly soul. "Excuse me, ma'm, but do you own a CB radio?"

"Yes, I do."

"Uh, do you know the rules regarding its proper operation?"

She waved a hand, as if shooing an insect. "Sure, sure I do. But those rules don't do me no good. Then I wouldn't be able to tell my story." She cackled laughter. "Had to pump up my power as it is. Four watts ain't nothing. I got a lot of friends out there."

"I'm sure you do," Spider said. "Nevertheless—"

"You got a name or something?" she interrupted.

"Uh, yes, ma'm. Blaine."

"Blaine who?"

"Lovejoy."

"You one of those Lovejoy boys?"

"Yes."

The old woman nodded. "I knew your mother. Barbara, right?"

"Yes, ma'm."

"Nice lady, nice lady. You say hello to her for me."

"She passed away many years ago," Spider said gently.

The old woman snorted. "I know that, honey. Give her my best."

Blaine promised he would and said good-bye.

Back in the car, he recounted the conversation for Cochise. "I couldn't do it. I mean, there was no way I could have gone in there and busted up her set."

Cochise looked sympathetic.

Spider scratched his head. "I'm thinking, though—I could cut her antenna wire. She doesn't really talk to people. She just broadcasts her story, never asks for a response. If I cut the wire, she'd probably never even know she was off the air."

Cochise rummaged in a canvas bag and withdrew a pair of wirecutters.

Spider got out and sidled furtively up to the side of the house and pussyfooted around the back, where the antenna wire ran out through a hole drilled in a window frame. He heard the old woman's voice droning on with her history.

He positioned the wirecutters, hesitated, then snipped the wire in two. The old woman continued her story happily.

Traffic was growing heavier with people on their way home from work. Spider concentrated on driving while Cochise monitored the signal finder.

A rasping voice from the CB read breathily: "When she was completely naked, except for her high-heeled patent-leather sandals and her black nylon stockings rolled down flat above her knees . . ."

Spider struck a fist against the steering wheel. "Jesus, I'd like to get him."

"Thirty degrees southeast," Cochise said.

Spider turned.

"Due east now," Cochise said.

"I had her kneel down, her back against the sofa, and to make her press more tightly against it with her shoulders than with her waist, I made her spread her thighs slightly. . . ."

Spider turned again.

"A tiny pearl of saliva appeared on the tip of her tongue, that luscious organ I wanted to . . ."

"Still due east," Cochise said, frowning.

Spider glanced at the map. "Damn! I think he's mobile."

". . . her skin shuddering deliciously beneath my feverish hand. . . ."

Spider turned again.

"Still due east," Cochise said.

Spider sighed. "He's mobile all right. Maybe he'll hit a base. . . ."

Hot Coffee was tooling down the highway thirty miles outside Union, feeling like the captain of a yacht in her new bright-red Winnebago. She was a hundred yards behind an eighteen-wheeler, its twin stacks belching out thin black smoke.

She picked up her CB mike and keyed it. "Hey, Short Stack. You got the ol' Hot Coffee. How 'bout some of that original hundred-mile perk-me-up that's sweet as sugar, full-bodied, and low on calories! Mercy! Come on back!"

A crackle of static preceded the reply. "'Preciate that offer, Hot Coffee, but I'm definitely doin' some serious motorin'. What's your twenty?"

Hot Coffee grinned. "Right on your donkey, partner! Right on your donkey!"

Ahead, she saw the driver's face appear in his side mirror as he glanced out.

She waved.

"I'm windin' down, mama!" came the voice from her radio.

The truck's right-hand directional lights came on, and the engine revved as the driver began shifting down through the gears. The truck eased over on the shoulder, slowed, then came to a stop. Hot Coffee pulled up behind. The truck door opened, and the driver jumped out. He came walking back with a big smile. Hot Coffee flashed her own pearly whites at him, and got out of her chair to open the door and spread the welcome mat.

In the phone booth at Texaco Jack's, Harold had his coin pouch out and stood with the receiver to his ear listening to the rings. On the tenth one, he flashed the operator.

His coins fell down into the return box.

"Yes?"

"Operator, could we try that Dallas number again, please?"

He fed the money into the slots again.

After the twelfth ring, the operator said, "I'm sorry sir, but your party doesn't answer."

"Okay. I'll try later. Thank you."

He collected his coins, puzzled. Connie should be there now. Oh, well. . . . He didn't have much to report anyway. He was still waiting for the axle.

Joyce had to change buses just over the Nebraska state line. The only service into Union was a feeder line. She walked into the terminal with a worn suitcase in either hand. It wasn't much. A small counter of steam trays, with a couple of tables waiting for the dirty dishes to be bused, rest rooms that could be smelled a dozen paces away, and some blue plastic chairs bolted together in lines along the walls.

She looked for an information booth. There wasn't any. And the line before the ticket window was long.

She sat down next to a pretty, younger woman with jet black hair wearing a prim dress that tried, but couldn't succeed, to mask her generous figure. The girl was reading a suspense novel.

"Excuse me," Joyce said, "but are we supposed to wait outside for the buses or do they announce them on the speakers?"

The girl set her novel aside. "They call us," she said in a friendly tone. "Where're you heading?"

"Union."

"Might as well settle in. We got an hour's wait."

"Oh, boy." Joyce took the scarf from her blonde hair, combed it out with her fingers. She stretched, making a little sound of pleasure. She hadn't been on a bus in years. She was into her late thirties, and the ride had cramped her.

"You got relatives in Union?" the dark-haired girl asked.

"Husband. I'm gonna surprise him."

"That's nice. Where're you from?"

"Iowa. Des Moines."

"I'm up from Dallas."

"I hear a lot about Dallas," Joyce said. "My husband's always going there."

"What's he do?"

"He's a trucker."

The dark-haired girl clapped her hands. "I knew it. I just knew it."

"Why do you say that?"

"'Cause it takes one to know one."

"You too?" Joyce said.

"Yup. I'm Connie," the girl said, extending her hand.

Joyce shook it. "Joyce."

"I just sensed it about you right away," Connie said. "I must have ESP or something. Same thing happened in a restaurant once. I said, 'That waitress is a trucker's wife.' I was right. How long you been together?"

"Twelve years."

"I've been ten. We must be setting some new kind of record."

"Do you think all those trucker articles they've been writing are true?"

Connie shrugged. "Some of it's true. But two things sure aren't. Truck-stop coffee tastes like pig shit—excuse my French—and truck-stop girls look like it."

"I decided long ago that you can think about it and worry and make your life miserable or just not think about it and hope for the best, which is what I do. Anyway, if I did find out that he was . . . unfaithful . . . I think I could deal with it. Golly, I've read enough articles about it in *Cosmopolitan*. I should be able to deal with it by now."

Connie assumed an expression of veteran knowledge. "Don't let those articles fool you. It's real hard. I know." She paused dramatically to light a cigarette. "I'll let you in on something. 'Bout two years ago I found out my husband . . . indulged . . . with a pavement princess. Don't ask me how I found out. I just did. Well, I waited a week for him to get home and I kept myself at full boil. Even sent the girls to my folks so they wouldn't be there when it happened. Well, I let him have it—cursing and slugging and crying and throwing things. Just like on TV. Then I locked myself away for two days, hoping he'd guilt himself to death. You know what happened? All of a sudden he starts being real nice to the boys, real buddy-buddy. Then he starts doing the dishes and things like that. He never did that before. Tippy-toeing around the house. Then, in the bedroom one night, all of a sudden he's by my side—" Here she dropped her voice to a conspirator's tone and arched her eyebrow significantly at Joyce. "Doing what all women like but no woman likes to mention. Before, I used to have to wait for my birthday. But it wasn't my birthday that night. And you know what?" She shook her head, as if wondering at herself. "I didn't have it in me to resist. Sure, I was hurting real bad. But I was lonely too. And I don't have to tell you what that loneliness does to you."

Joyce nodded. "That's for sure."

"The next morning I hear his truck start up and he's gone for another few weeks. I don't know what to think. So I think about the laundry. Then I think about the plumber coming to fix the bathroom faucets. I just let the day sorta pull me along." She sighed. "They've been pulling me along ever since."

Joyce shook her head. "Maybe *you* should be writing those articles." She wrinkled her forehead, thinking. "Do you still love him?"

Connie laughed. "I figure if I don't ask myself that I won't get into trouble." She rummaged in her purse. "Here's some pictures of the girls."

"My husband always wanted a girl," Joyce said wistfully, taking the photos. "But we got three boys. He wanted to try again, but I said no. After three times, the fun's out of it, you know? I think it's a sore point between us." She held the photos up and looked at them admiringly. "Gee, they're a couple of cuties."

She passed the pictures back, produced a couple of her own. "Here's some of our boys. Jim, Chris, and Mike. That's our house in the back."

"They look just like you," Connie said, thumbing through the half dozen photos.

"Christy and Nan have their father's eyes and mouth."

Connie stopped and stared at the last photo. Her forehead furrowed. "Did I just give you this one?"

"No," Joyce said, puzzled.

"Are you sure?" A slow, stunned expression was spreading over Connie's face.

"Sure I'm sure. That's my husband, Harold."

"Oh, sweet Jesus!" Connie gasped.

"What's the matter?"

Connie shook her head. "Oh, we've got a lot in common, honey. We've got a whole truckload in common." She picked another photo from the bottom of her purse and passed it without comment to Joyce.

Joyce glanced at it, did a double take, held Connie's photo up next to her own.

"Oh, no!"

The photos were twin shots of Harold, the Chrome Angel, standing in front of his gleaming Kenworth, hands on his hips, a great grin on his mouth.

Tears popped into Joyce's eyes. "D-Does this," she stammered, "does this mean we're related?"

CHAPTER 10

Spider pulled up alongside the workshop.

The Priest was broadcasting. "Children," he intoned, "honor thy father and thy mother. Such is the first commandment with a promise—that it may be well with thee, and that thou mayest be long-lived upon the earth. Fathers, do not provoke your children to anger, but rear them in the discipline and admonition of the Lord. Now is that a four?"

Spider flicked the set off. He didn't have time for the Priest, or for Triple-X, or for any of them. He sprinted into the house.

"You ready, Pop?" he yelled as he banged through the door. "We've only got fifteen minutes to make it to the hall."

He stopped abruptly. Floyd Lovejoy was collapsed over the table, head on his arms, an empty bottle of Old Crow beside him. His unshaven cheeks twitched, his mouth worked, and he mumbled almost inaudibly. A rumbling belch burst past his lips, and a thunderous blast shot from his opposite orifice.

His CB set, volume turned low, murmured and sputtered behind him.

Spider's mouth went hard. "Terrific, Pop. You couldn't wait another hour. Not another god-damned hour."

He stalked into his bedroom, changed his pants and shirt in a hurry, threw a tie around his neck, grabbed a sport coat and hung it in the crook of his arm, and returned to the kitchen, knotting the tie and drawing it up.

"I can't tell you how proud this makes me feel," he said to his comatose father.

He lifted the empty bottle and banged it down on the table a few inches from Floyd's head. Floyd slurred something incomprehensible, but made no other response.

"Real proud, Pop. Real proud," Spider said bitterly. He got into his jacket and went to the door and opened it. He paused a moment to look back. He said, "One of these days, good buddy. . . ."

The game was in its final moments. The Union team was trailing by two points. The Edgetown team had the ball and the fans went wild (this being Edgetown's home court) as they drove down the floor toward the Union basket.

Then suddenly a Union man stole the ball away from Edgetown's forward in mid-dribble, and the players reversed themselves, battling in mid-court for possession.

Dean Lovejoy stalked up and down in front of the Union bench on the sidelines. He wore a blue

blazer and a tie, but the knot of his tie was drawn
down several inches and his collar button was
open. He was chewing gum maniacally and
pounding a fist into his palm.

"Let's go, let's go, let's go!" he screamed. "Who's
your man, Webber? Who's your man? Well, come
on then! Watch the pick! *The pick!*"

Edgetown regained the ball.

"Aw, Christ!" Dean bellowed. He grabbed a
towel from the bench, flung it down in disgust,
and kicked it.

But then his boys snatched the ball back again
and he leaped straight up in the air.

"That's it! That's it! All right! Yeah! Yeah!
Yeah!"

The substitute buzzer blatted. The players
huddled. The Union cheerleaders jumped off the
first row of seats and went into action. They did
a series of jumps and cartwheels, firm thighs
flashing under abbreviated little skirts and nubile
breasts bouncing, then led the Union fans in a
cheer:

> "Two bits, four bits,
>   Six bits, a dollar!
>   All for Union
>   Stand up and holler!"

The Union fans stood and roared.

Dean turned and faced them and raised his
hands in a double victory sign. His eyes fell mo-
mentarily on Pam, who was seated in the upper
tier alongside one of her cheerleaders, who was
out of commission with a sprained ankle. Pam
looked glum, which wasn't like her at all.

The whistle blew and Dean whirled back to

the court, cupped his hands to his mouth, and screamed, "All right! All right! Let's go! Let's go!"

There was a quick flurry. Union scored. The game was tied and the Union fans ran amok. The clock ticked off the remaining seconds as the Edgetown team ran the ball down court—five, four, three, two—and their forward lofted the ball in a desperation shot, and the buzzer sounded as it was in air, and it went through the net slick as a whistle, and Edgetown won, 108 to 106.

"Aw, shit!" Dean said. And tears rose to his eyes. He was a man who took his games very seriously.

In the Union bus forty-five minutes later, Dean made a head count of his players, and Pam checked to see that her cheerleaders were all there. Then they took their seats in the front of the bus, behind the driver.

The engine turned over. The driver shifted with a grinding of gears, and the bus lurched forward, leaving behind a foul bluish cloud of exhaust in the moonlit night.

They rode in silence several minutes.

Then Dean, who accepted his defeats manfully once the initial shock had passed, said to Pam, "You're very quiet tonight. Is anything wrong?"

"No."

He reached and took her hand, patted it affectionately. "I guess losing is never easy," he counseled. "But you've got to look on the positive side. Tomorrow is a new ball game. On the other hand, none of us takes it well at first." He jerked his head toward the back of the bus. "Listen how quiet it is back there. It gets them down too."

Pam turned. "Take a look at how down they are," she said with faint amusement.

Dean swiveled his head around.

Every available cheerleader was wrapped up in the panting embrace of a player. A professional contortionist would have envied the positions into which they'd managed to get themselves in the limited space of the seats. Those players not lucky enough to have one of the girls looked on in intense, envious attention. The rear windows had begun to steam up.

"Harumph! Harumph!" Dean went noisily. "Excuse me, ladies and gentlemen, but can we have a little discretion tonight? Thank you."

Dean turned back without checking to see that his request had been honored. He didn't expect that it would be. And that was embarrassing. So it was better to act as if he'd been obeyed. Pam went along with the charade.

When they reached the Union school, they bade goodnight to the players.

The American Legion Hall was a one-story, shedlike building resembling an old Grange Hall. Inside, the floors were covered with vinyl tile and the walls with high-gloss imitation wood paneling. There were two long tables at which sat a bored compendium of dentists, businessmen, and insurance salesmen, warriors whose golden days had turned to gray and whose dreams had settled into their paunches.

The mayor, a heavy-jowled man, stood at the podium finishing his introduction, glancing at Spider, seated in a flanking chair, as he spoke.

"This young man is no stranger to us. We've honored him before and I suspect we'll do it again. It's getting to be a habit, but a good one. Recently, Blaine helped save the life of a stranded trucker while operating an Emergency React station at his own volition and expense. It gives me great pleasure to present this Distinguished Citizen Award to Blaine Lovejoy for the bravery, courage, and decency that we hope will serve as a model for all our citizens. Blaine!"

Blaine stood up, acknowledging the scattered applause with an embarrassed nod. The mayor placed a ribbon and medallion over his head. They shook hands.

"Congratulations, Blaine."

"Thank you," Spider said.

"Thank *you* for the good work."

"Thank you," Spider repeated uncomfortably.

Dinner was a desultory creamed chicken on toast. Spider ate alone. The seat to his right had been reserved for the mayor, but the mayor had had to leave for an urgent appointment with the city comptroller. The seat on his left had been designated for Floyd, who, of course, was still sleeping it off on the kitchen table.

Spider picked at the tasteless food, waiting for the ordeal to end. By the time coffee was served, the Legionnaires were clustering into small groups, and many were heading for the exits.

A man in a double-knit suit sidled up to Spider, then plopped into the chair at his side and extended his hand.

"Blaine, Bob Ames," he said heartily. "Congratulations. This must be a big moment for you."

Blaine nodded politely.

"Another big moment," Ames instructed, "is the decision to purchase a life insurance plan. Have you given that any thought?"

Spider shook his head negatively.

"I work with a company that specializes in policies for promising young men like yourself," Ames said confidentially. "Believe me, it's something you should start thinking about."

Spider nodded believingly.

Ames removed a business card from his wallet. "I know this isn't the time or place, so take this, and, when you're ready, give me a shout and we'll sit down in private and work something out. We also specialize in auto insurance, home owner's, medical—you name it. Well, nice talking with you, Blaine. And congratulations."

Spider nodded. Ames rose and wandered off.

Spider felt that courtesy required him to remain through the Jell-O dessert. He did, then made his way out, shaking the few bored hands that were thrust at him as he moved toward the exit.

When he got home, Floyd was still dead to the world at the table. Spider opened a can of Mighty Dog, feeling the creamed chicken curdle in his stomach at the smell, and fed Ned. Ned knocked over his water dish and slipped spread-eagled to the floor in his happy haste to reach the stuff, and laid there eating on his belly, tail thumping rhythmically.

Spider went into his bedroom, shucked out of his dinner clothes, and got into Levis and a comfortable flannel shirt again. He opened his bureau drawer and went to place the medal within it. There were five identical ones there already. He looked at them, reflectively pushing out his cheek with his tongue. With a quick move, he snatched them all up and went back to the kitchen. One by one he dropped each of them into the empty Mighty Dog can, exciting Ned, then dropped the can into the garbage, disappointing the mutt.

"You can't eat them anyway," he said.

The dog didn't believe him and stared mournfully at the garbage.

Spider looked at his snoring father. "Aw, shit, Pop," he said softly. "Aw, shit."

He dug his car keys out of his pocket and went outside.

In a while, he found himself passing a darkened shopping plaza. He turned into the empty parking lot on impulse, and he began to drive round and round in tight little circles, trying to blank his mind, round and round and round. . . .

Spider found himself in the school parking lot, leaning against his fender, waiting for the bus to return from the Edgetown game.

It arrived, and a couple of cheerleaders exited first, followed by Pam.

He went up to her and took her arm. "We've got to talk," he said.

She pulled her arm away and walked toward the school with her girls.

"Okay, guys, let's go, let's go," said Dean, who was still in the bus, hustling his players out.

Spider waved to him. "Hey, Dean! See you in the morning, huh?"

Dean acknowledged him with a nod.

Spider went after Pam. He caught up with her halfway into the gym.

"How ya doin'?" he said.

"It's late, Blaine."

"I know, but this is important. I've decided to —hey, slow down."

"Can't this wait?"

"I've decided to leave the Funny Farm. I'm leaving Pop to himself. Will you stop a minute?"

She did. "It's so late."

"Maybe you're right. I've been sitting out here for over an hour freezing my buns off waiting for you thinking about how late it was getting. I knew it was late, but I had no idea it was *so late.*"

He turned to leave.

She touched his arm. "Blaine . . ."

He paused.

She worried her lip, then inclined her head toward a door. "In there, the ballet room. It's private. We can talk."

Spider followed her in.

"When did you tell Floyd?"

"I didn't."

Pam grew indignant. "Then what *is* all this, Blaine Lovejoy?"

"I said I'm *going* to tell him. After his birthday party. I'll tell him then."

Pam settled down again. "Do you think he can take care of himself? You said he was getting senile."

Spider curled his mouth wryly. "Yeah, well, he gets senile like some people get the flu. He had a bad bout last month, but he's over it now. He's much better. Hey, this is what you wanted, isn't it? This is what hung us up. Remember, you said I was so busy saving lives to impress my father that I was losing my own. Remember? Isn't this what you wanted?"

Pam lowered her eyes. "That's what I wanted, Blaine. But that was three months ago. Things have changed."

"You still have my ring."

"I tried to give it back," Pam reminded him.

"If you don't mind me saying so, I think I probably know you better than anyone else, and if things have changed as much as you say they have, then you wouldn't be as unhappy as you are right now, so the way I see it, things haven't changed all that much. Am I wrong? Tell me, am I so wrong about that?"

Pam forced a smile. She wasn't very successful.

"All right, then, goddamnit, let's face up to our feelings," Spider said.

Pam turned to leave, but Spider stopped her. He kissed her lightly, awkwardly, catching her cheek. He pulled her in, kissed her again, full on the mouth this time, palms sliding down her back, chest meeting and flattening her breasts, hips coming against hers. She molded herself to him a moment. Then they drew back, smiling at each other uncertainly. She took his hand up, kissed it, and turned quickly and left him alone.

When Dean had gotten all his boys off the bus he went down into the locker room to try to cheer them up.

"Good hustle tonight, Bosley. Ken, you wanna take care of the warm-ups?"

Richie Webber was sitting on a bench, ashen-faced, head hanging, tears brimming in his eyes. Dean went over to him and put a hand on his shoulder.

"It's all right, Webber."

"No, sir. It's not all right." Richie's voice cracked.

"Well, Webber, tell me this—are you gonna be a man about this thing and accept your mistakes and learn from them, or are you gonna sit there like a little bunny all night punishing yourself?"

Richie didn't respond.

"Tell you what," Dean said with a smile. "Give me twenty in the morning and we'll call it even."

But Richie only went deeper into his unhappiness.

"Okay, Webber, enough's enough. I want you to pop your fanny into the shower and I want you to soap up good and I want you back here smiling. Now!"

Sluggishly, Webber began stripping down.

Dean turned and started to walk away.

"Coach . . ." Webber said quietly behind him, "it's not all right."

Dean shook his head sadly. He went out of the locker room and up the stairs to look for Pam.

When he found her, he wished he hadn't—she was in Spider's arms in the ballet room, her lithe body pressed to his, and their mouths locked together. He paused, dumbstruck, outside the partly open door, then he tore himself away and walked quickly down the hall, his hand rising to swipe at the moisture that leaped to his eyes.

CHAPTER 11

SPIDER WAS IN HIS WORKSHOP, GATHERING UP the new batch of CBs he'd repaired for CB-er's Haven.

Triple-X's voice blared out of his own set: "Hey there! This is the ol' Triple-X! Sorry I had to be away for a while, but we'll pick right back up where we left off. Remember, he had a gun on her and he just forced her to take all the clothes off that yummy body of hers. Here goes. So I fastened the collar and bracelets to her neck and wrists and told her to get up. I took her place on the fur ottoman, called her over till she was touching my knees, and slipped my hand between—"

Spider clicked the set dead. "Screw off, jerk!"

He carried the radios out to the Nomad and put them in the trunk. Then he went into the house to tell his father he was on his way into town.

Floyd had his CB on the kitchen table. He sat before it with a cup of coffee, staring at it, waiting for it to talk to him.

Ned the Dog was amusing himself by walking around the kitchen in circles.

"Pop," Spider said. "Don't forget about our guest today."

Floyd continued to stare at his set, as if he could will a voice from it.

"I'm leaving Ned here until lunch," Spider said. "I've too many errands to run."

"Then the dog dies," Floyd said without looking up.

Spider, out of patience, said, "Do whatever you want. I'm leaving him here."

Spider drove into town. He dropped the radios off, picked up the new ones, then went over to the bakery on Christopher Street. Dean was already there, waiting for him.

"Hey, Dean. How's it going?"

Dean nodded, his face gloomy.

"You look down," Spider said. "Anything wrong?"

For a moment, Dean looked as if he were about to say something, then he shook his head. "No. Nothing. Just off my feed, I guess."

They went inside and asked for the birthday cakes. The shop girl led them to a refrigerated counter with nearly two dozen cakes of various sizes and gaudiness, some topped with little figurines—cowboys, spacemen, sports players.

"Do you see any you like?" Spider asked.

"I don't care."

"I'm asking your opinion, Dean."

"I said I don't care. It's your party. You choose."

"Goddamnit! It's not my party. It's our party. Now which goddamn cake do you like the best?"

"That one," Dean said, pointing arbitrarily.

"Okay." He said to the salesgirl. "We'll take the white one, please. With red trim. Skip the flowers."

The girl wrote it down.

"That sound all right, Dean?"

"Fine."

"And I'd like it to say, 'Happy Birthday, Pop,'" Spider said to the girl.

Dean looked up. "I never called him Pop."

"Well, what do you want it to say?"

"I don't care. I just never called him Pop, that's all."

"Okay, make that, 'Happy Birthday, Dad.'"

The girl used her eraser, then penciled in the new salutation.

"I never called him Dad either," Dean said.

"What'd ya want," Spider said in exasperation, "'Happy Birthday, Shithead'?"

The girl winced.

"Dad's fine," he said to her. "Now, have you got any little trucks? I'd like some little trucks, some little trucks driving up a highway. Can you do the highway in perspective? With broken white lines?"

"I guess so."

"Good. Little trucks driving up a highway in perspective with broken white lines. He'll like that. But no flowers. You always wind up throwing the flowers away. Okay?"

"Got it," the girl said, scribbling on her pad. She started backing toward the swinging doors, beyond which was the kitchen, anxious to be rid of this pair.

On the street again, Spider said, "I think he'll like it."

"Sure," Dean said without interest.

"You sure something isn't eating you?"

"I'm sure."

"Well . . . okay. I'll see you at the party, then, huh?"

"Sure."

They turned in separate directions for their cars.

Spider picked Pam up and drove her out to the Funny Farm. She stood leaning against the Nomad while he went in to check on things.

"It's like a big mystery," he said. "You never know what kind of shape he's going to be in when you get home."

He was gone a few minutes, then he came back out for her. "Everything's fine," he said, with some surprise. "He's even made lunch for us."

"I didn't know he cooked," Pam said, linking her arm in his and walking up the steps with him.

"He doesn't," Spider said, baffled.

Floyd was at the stove, stirring a murky stew in a big pot.

"Smells great, Pop!" Spider said.

Floyd didn't say anything.

Three places were set at the table. Spider and Pam sat down.

Floyd ladled the stew into three bowls and carried them over. He sat down wtih them and waited for them to taste.

Pam looked down with some reservation at the stringy gristle-clogged meat in the stew, but she smiled and said, "Well, shall we?" She picked up her fork.

Spider picked up his. "I didn't know we had any meat in the house, Pop. Did you go shopping?"

"No," Floyd said.

Spider put a piece into his mouth. He chewed with effort.

Pam, hesitating, looked to him for a reaction.

There was none. Reaching for the salt, Spider allowed his napkin to slide from his lap onto the floor. He bent over to pick it up. As he did, he whispered to Pam, "Don't eat it. It tastes like horsemeat."

"Dogmeat," Floyd said loudly.

"What?"

"You said horsemeat."

"Yeah?"

"Dogmeat."

Spider stared into his bowl. The color drained from his face. He snapped his eyes up and looked frantically around the kitchen.

"Pop," he said in alarm. "Where's Ned?"

Floyd smiled broadly, looking smug and pleased with himself.

"Oh, God," said Pam.

Spider jumped to his feet, tipping his chair over on the floor. "Pop, where's Ned?"

Floyd stirred his fork around in his bowl and chortled.

Spider ran outside. They could hear him crying, "Ned! Ned! Ned!" He rushed about the yard, and into the garage, the truck skeletons, the workshop.

Floyd forked stew meat into his mouth, chewing with relish and chuckling to himself.

Pam stared at him, not trusting herself to say a word. Gingerly she lifted a piece of meat from her bowl. She turned it over, examining it. She placed a corner between her teeth and nibbled at it, then popped the whole piece in, chewed and swallowed.

"He's a little tough," she said to Floyd. "Did you simmer him long enough?"

Floyd's mirth ceased. He met Pam's eyes, defiant.

"I've found dachshund to be more tender. And quite tasty actually," Pam said.

They faced each other as unmoving and belligerently as opposing chess pieces. Then, very slowly, Floyd smiled. Pam returned his smile.

Floyd leaned back in his chair and grasped the knob of the closet door to his side. He opened and pulled.

"How ya doin', moose breath?"

Ned, who was curled up on an old piece of rug on the closet floor, opened his eyes, raised his head a little and went, "Blurrf?" Then his head sank back down, he stretched with a sigh, and curled up and went back to sleep again.

"You see how I live?" Floyd said, with some challenge in his voice. "In a junk yard. I know that as well as anyone. I worked all my life to end up living in a junk yard. See? This country promises everything, sure, but you never see any of it. Hah, you bet your ass you don't. Did you ever see any of it?" he demanded.

Pam shrugged.

"I should o' stayed in Canada. Dumb Floyd, that's what I call me. Could o' had a cattle ranch there. But the missus wanted the boys raised Americans. Big deal. I could o' had cattle. I could o' been someone. Look what I got." He spread his arms wide. "A lot of rusty doodoos. You look smart. If you're smart, you'll go to Canada. It's just north from here. On the other side of the woods. I'd go, but I gotta stay for him." He jerked his head out toward the yard, where Spider was still calling for Ned. "I promised the missus."

He looked down at his bowl again. His shoulders sagged. He nodded to himself.

Spider came in. He leaned wearily against the door frame. His face was ashen.

"He did it. He really did it," he said to Pam.

Pam got up and walked to the closet. She opened the door. Spider's eyes widened.

Taking Pam back home after lunch, Spider laughed and shook his head. "Yeah, one thing about Pop," he said, "he really enjoys a joke. And the thing is, he likes it when you play along with him like I did. Sort of makes him feel good. That's why I went out into the yard like that."

Pam glanced at him in amusement, but he didn't notice.

"It's just great the way he still gets a kick out of it," Spider said, slapping his thigh. "Just great. I'll bet he had you faked out real good."

"Right out of my socks," Pam said.

"Yeah. The old buzzard sure enjoys a good joke." He looked out the driver's-side window and muttered to himself, "That fucker!" Then, eyes ahead once more, he said heartily, "Yes, sir."

Harold and Hot Coffee were cruising around the periphery of Union in Hot Coffee's new Winnebago for the sheer pleasant hell of it. They had vodka tonics in their hands, and there was a rollicking country-western tape on the wall-mounted player in the living room behind them. It was a gas, sitting down with a friend in the privacy of that friend's home and watching the sights roll by at a steady 40 miles per hour.

"I gotta hand it to you," Hot Coffee said. "It works like a charm. Should've thought of it long ago."

"How's it drive?"

"Slicker'n the hair on a patent medicine sales-man."

Idly, Harold looked out the window. His jaw dropped as if he'd been whacked in the back of the head with a baseball bat.

Suitcases in hand, he saw his wife Joyce and his wife Connie walking across from the bus sta-tion to the Stop-Rite Motel just across the street.

He slid down in his seat like a turtle pulling in its head. "Punch out, Debbie!"

"What?"

"Just punch out," he said desperately. "Step on it!"

Hot Coffee stomped the accelerator to the floor, and the Winnebago sprang forward.

"What's wrong?"

"There's something I haven't told you," Harold said, as the Stop-Rite Motel dropped back behind them.

"What's that?"

"As soon as we put some miles under us."

After they'd checked in (they were agitated briefly over whether or not to share a room, but in the end decided there was something perverse about that, and, relieved, took a pair of singles) and freshened up, they went down together to the motel's restaurant.

"I'll buy," Connie said as they studied the menus.

"I can't let you do that."

"Sugar," Connie said reassuringly, "I won't be paying for it. I'm putting it on Harold's charge account. This one's on him."

"Well . . . okay, then."

The waitress appeared.

Connie tapped a long-nailed finger on an entry. "Is this steak the most expensive thing you've got?"

"Yes, ma'm."

"What a shame. It's only $6.95. Should we make that two, Joyce?"

Joyce looked a little troubled, but she consented.

"And I'd like to see your wine list too," Connie said.

The waitress left.

Joyce fidgeted with her napkin. "I think we should be very careful what we say to each other."

"Why?"

"Because there might be litigation. And with litigation, you're not supposed to talk about anything."

Connie reflected, then said, "Perhaps you're right."

The waitress returned with the wine list. Connie didn't bother with the names, she went right to the prices, and ordered the costliest, a $15 bottle of St. Emilion. She tasted the wine when it came, and it was terrific, and she intended to enjoy every last drop of it.

"Can I ask you something?" Joyce said.

"Go ahead."

"Why did you come here?"

"He called and said his truck broke down," Connie said. "I didn't believe him."

"*I* thought he was hurt. I thought he might need me." Joyce made a sound deriding her own naiveté. "Do you think there are others? Besides us?"

"I don't know how there could be. The man's got a heart murmur. He can only do so much."

"He does? I didn't know that."

"Born with it," Connie said.

"Maybe he's got another woman here. A mistress."

Connie snorted. "Now that would really irk my quirk. I mean, seeing another wife is one thing. But seeing another woman is a whole different ball of wax."

"Am I that . . . other woman you found out about?"

"I don't know."

"Then, for all we know, he really hasn't been unfaithful—technically speaking."

This was a very tricky concept. Connie couldn't handle it right off the bat. "Let me set on that one for a while."

"What kind of ceremony did you have?"

"Episcopal."

"We had Methodist," Joyce said.

"You're Methodist?"

"No, I'm Catholic. He wanted it Methodist."

"He did?"

"That's how we're raising the little ones."

"You are? I'll be damned. Let me see that picture again."

Joyce got the photo out and gave it to Connie. Connie held it up and squinted at it.

"He sure looks like the same man."

"Same truck too," Joyce said. Her eyes took on a dreamy, faraway look. "I've always loved that truck. . . ."

CHAPTER 12

HAROLD TOLD HER THE STORY ON THE WAY OUT of Union.

Hot Coffee pulled the Winnebago off the road into a rest area, a pleasant sunny space in a pine grove along the banks of a lazy creek.

Harold dumped the remainder of his drink down the kitchen sink. "I got to function on all cylinders," he said.

Hot Coffee made coffee for them and they sat at the kitchen table. Harold stared out at the creek morosely.

"Do you think they're talking about me?" he said.

"There's a good chance of that—yes."

"Christ, this is embarrassing."

"I suspect it might be—yes."

"I'll tell you one thing," Harold said, like Nathan Hale getting ready to swing. "I don't regret what I've done for one minute. Not for one minute. They're good women and I love them both."

Hot Coffee thought about this. "I'm not sure that's going to help you much," she said.

The table between Connie and Joyce was cluttered with the plates from their meal, and those from the appetizers, and those from the lavish desserts. They were halfway into their second bottle of wine.

"You mean," Connie said, a little fuzzily, "that first he'd kiss you, then he'd take off your clothes, then he'd set you on the bed, and *then* he'd take off his shorts?"

Joyce shook her head. "No. First he'd take off my clothes, then he'd kiss me, then he'd take off his shorts, and *then* he'd set me on the bed."

"Then what?"

Joyce went a little coy and giggly. "Then he'd say, 'Babes, sometimes I'm on the road so long, I forget how soft a woman really feels.'"

"Oh, shit."

"He says the same thing to you, huh?"

"Exactly," Connie said, depressed.

"I don't know if we should be talking like this. It seems . . . I don't know . . . kind of weird, you know?"

"Sometimes," Harold said earnestly to Hot Coffee, "when you're on the road for a long time, you forget how soft a woman really feels."

"I know," she said skeptically. "You've told me."

"All right. I'll admit it." Harold threw up his hands. "My gonads have run away with my life.

But don't think I don't know that. I tried to make the best of it under the circumstances. I mean, a man's got to feel like a man, don't he? I don't regret any of it. I'm willing to take the responsibility. I'm willing to take a little heat." He took her hands in his and gazed into her eyes. "Debbie, tell me, what do I do?"

"Talk to them. See how they feel."

Harold winced at the prospect. "You're my best friend. Will you go with me?"

"You're not afraid, are you?"

"Hell, no! I just want you there. Just in case."

Joyce and Connie were a little unsteady on their feet as they made their way down the hall toward their rooms.

"Did you ever read any articles about those friendly kinds of divorces people are getting today?" Connie said.

Joyce nodded sadly.

"You know the ones. The couples are real nice to each other during the whole thing. Then afterwards they still see each other like friends. . . . Some of them even go out on dates."

Joyce nodded sadly.

Connie lifted her chin. "I'm gonna have me one of those friendly divorces. But first I'm gonna bust his balls. I just wanted you to know. . . ."

"What do we do now?"

"Find him. Find him, bust his balls, then divorce him."

Joyce looked uncertain.

"Well," Connie said in a somewhat softer tone. "First we find him anyway."

Spider and Cochise sat in the darkness in

Spider's Nomad on a street of rundown houses. The one that occupied their particular attention was a dilapidated structure with shutters hanging at angles, a half-collapsed porch, and an unkempt yard. Rising up from the roof was a tall towerlike antenna that looked like it should be part of the Early Warning System.

From the CB came the Nazi's voice: "Yeah, you got to admit, ol' Hitler was right. He was a good ol' boy. Oil and water don't mix, that's for peapickin' sure. Maybe this ol' country ain't pure yet, but this channel's sure gonna be."

Spider stared out through the window at the huge antenna. "Cochise, my man, you're looking at two thousand watts of pure radio power. One thousand, nine hundred and ninety-six of them are illegal."

"So if any of you peapickers want in here," the Nazi said, "you just ask me, and if I like the sound of your voice—or the color of it—I just might let you in. How's that?"

Spider said, "Why is it that the smallest minds always have the biggest antennas?"

He sighed and got out of the car. He cut across the lawn, mounted the steps to the crumbling porch, and knocked on the door.

A slab-shouldered man in a grimy T-shirt answered. He wore his blond hair in a stiff crew cut. His arms were hairy and long and muscled, and a big blue swastika was tattooed on one of them. His gut lipped over the waist of his pants.

"Yeah?" he growled.

On sudden inspiration, Spider whipped out his wallet and flashed it open and closed—allowing the briefest glimpse of his volunteer fireman's shield—then jammed it back in his pocket.

"I'm with the Federal Communications Commission," he said. "We've had numerous complaints concerning your use of a CB radio."

"What?" the Nazi roared.

"Uh, illegal antenna," Spider said, trying to keep his voice from cracking. "Illegal power. You're bleeding over four channels and won't allow anyone in without your permission."

"That's right, Jack," the Nazi snarled.

Taking a deep breath to bolster his courage, Spider slipped past the man into the dingy entrance hall. "May I see your equipment, please?"

"What's this—Communism right here?"

"Do you have a license?"

"Yeah." The man turned to a telephone table. "In the drawer here."

Spider waited.

The man whipped around with a nickel-plated revolver and shoved it up painfully against Spider's neck. "Here's my peapickin' license, Jack! In .38 caliber. What else you want to see?"

"Uh," Spider said. "Uh. . . . Would you mind moving that a little to the side, sir? It's, uh, pressing against my jugular vein and becoming uncomfortable."

"Out!" the Nazi ordered. "Out!"

Spider backed through the door onto the porch, the Nazi following, the gun still pressed into Spider's flesh.

"Uh," Spider said. "I think that'll be all for tonight. Thank you, sir."

The Nazi slammed the door in his face.

Back in the Nomad, Spider, the thudding of his heart only now beginning to subside, said to Cochise, "This could be more difficult than I thought."

They conferred, then waited several more minutes, until the Nazi went on the air again and they were sure he wasn't keeping watch. Then they took a long coil of thick rope from the trunk and snuck back to the house. Spider tied one end of the rope to the rear bumper of the man's car, which sat in the driveway in front of the garage, nose pointing toward the street. They went to the side of the garage.

"Give me a boost up," Spider whispered.

Cochise locked his hands together. Spider hung the rest of the rope around his shoulder and put a foot into Cochise's hands. Cochise heaved him up, Spider caught hold of the rain gutter, and swung himself atop the garage. From there he made his way to the roof of the house and to the base of the antenna. He climbed halfway up the antenna and tied the other end of the rope to it.

Below, Cochise craned his head back to watch. The angle was sharp and caused a pain in his neck. He stepped backward, out from the garage and into the front yard. Something hard, about the size of a nickle, pressed into his back. He froze, fearful that he knew precisely what the object was.

"Turn around slow, peapicker," came a rasping voice.

Cochise did, and stared haplessly into the muzzle of a rifle. Behind the rifle was the Nazi.

"You're the biggest fucking Commie I ever saw," the Nazi said, his voice like a file rasping over metal.

"Spider!" Cochise cried.

On the roof, Spider cut the last of the antenna's four stabilizing wires and tiptoed over to where he could look down into the yard.

"Spiii-der!" Cochise wailed.

"What is that—some kind of code?" the Nazi said suspiciously. He darted his eyes around the yard.

Spider launched himself into the air. He came down on the Nazi's back, knocking him to the ground and sending the rifle spinning away. They thrashed about together like hooked fish. Through sheer luck, Spider managed to get a headlock on the man. But that didn't subdue him much. He threw his muscular body about and punched at Spider with hammerlike blows.

"Cochise," Spider gasped. "Jump on him!"

Cochise was terrified, and paralyzed.

"*Jump on him!*" Spider yelled.

Cochise twitched, made a face of great dismay, then leaped up in the air and came down with his immense bulk sprawled across the man's back.

The Nazi's eyes distended and his breath rushed out of him with a loud *whoosh*.

Spider sprang to his feet and helped Cochise up. The Nazi writhed on the ground in breathless agony. Spider searched frantically until he found the rifle, then picked it up and threw it to the roof.

"Let's haul ass!" he said.

They ran back to the Nomad, Cochise lumbering elephantlike with a rolling gait.

Spider started the Nomad. The Nazi was up on his knees, struggled to his feet. He reached into his pants pocket and pulled out the nickel-plated revolver.

Spider put the Nomad in gear and burned a little rubber, but slowed once he was out of pistol range. They turned their heads back to watch.

The Nazi staggered to his car. The engine roared to life.

"Get ready. . . ." Spider said.

The Nazi tromped his accelerator. The car shot forward, then came to a jarring halt. There was a loud groaning and wrenching as the giant antenna was pulled loose from its moorings. It came toppling down ever so slowly and crashed into the driveway, breaking apart, and bounced once before it settled into a smashed wreck.

The Nazi jumped out of his car, glanced at the ruin of his antenna and screamed in rage. He spun around, spotted the Nomad, and charged toward it.

"Uh, Spider. . . ." Cochise said nervously as the man neared.

"Okay," Spider said.

He hit the gas. The engine sputtered, revved, backfired, and went dead.

Spider twisted the key, grinding the starter.

The Nazi was within twenty yards and running hard.

"Uh, Spider. . . ."

The engine caught just as the Nazi came abreast of the Nomad and reached for the door.

Spider roared away. The Nazi, driven by blind fury, kept after them.

Cochise sighed with relief as they drew away from him.

Then the Nomad slowed. The Nazi gained fast.

"What in God's name are you doing?" Cochise yelled.

"Stop sign," Spider said, nodding ahead.

He pulled away again, accelerating. Cochise watched through the back window until the Nazi was lost in the night behind them.

"Spider," he said. "I'm sorry, but I don't think I like this anymore."

They drove to the other side of town and stopped at a hamburger joint. They ate with good appetites. The food calmed Cochise down and made Spider reflective.

"You know," Spider said. "I was just a kid when Mom died. But I figured it wouldn't be too bad because she'd talk to me over Channel Twelve— that was our lucky number. So late at night, when everyone was sleeping, I'd turn my CB to Twelve, real low, and wait. Nothing happened for a while. But then I heard this woman breathing hard and I figured it must be Mom because that's how she sounded when she was sick. So I'd say, 'Mom, this is Blaine. Mom, this is Blaine. Over.' I'd get the same breathing, only now she'd be crying and moaning too. I figured, jeez, maybe she misses me so much, it hurts her just to hear my voice. I'd listen a little more, but when the crying and moaning got too loud, I'd have to shut it off. It killed me to hear it. I'd shake and cry under the covers for hours." Spider looked down at his hands. He laughed once, bitterly. "It turned out there was some weird guy who kept his mike keyed while he balled his wife. There I was, just a kid, crying my heart out, but all the time it was just this lady coming like a freight train. . . ."

Cochise had a Coke glass to his mouth. He exploded in laughter, splattering Coke across the table.

"That's the funniest story!" he guffawed.

"You like that one?" Spider said, sadly, without anger.

"You're the funniest guy!" Cochise said.

It was a little past midnight when Spider got home. He was feeling moody and not sleepy, so he went out to his workship and started tinkering with the sets he'd picked up from CB-er's Haven.

His own set, as usual, was monitoring Emergency React.

He'd been working half an hour when a gruff, male voice sounded: "How 'bout it, React? You got a copy?"

Spider picked up his mike.

"This is KKT6757, Union React. Go ahead."

"I'm lookin' for that Spider."

"Go."

"Want some advice, Spider? Stay on that Funny Farm if you know what's good for you."

"Who is this?" Spider said.

"Or you just might get your britches dusted and your lights punched out."

"You're scaring me," Spider said. "Who is this?"

"We know who you are, where you are, what you are, and how to get you."

"You got a name, Bozo?"

"They call me Blood. And we just might spill yours all over the sidewalk."

"Real good, Blood. Nice talking with you. You're a real idiot. Say hello to Santa's little helpers for me."

With a savage twist of his hand, Spider turned off his radio.

CHAPTER 13
|||||||||||||||||||||||||||||||||||||||||||||||||||||||||||||||||||||||

IT WAS LATE. THE DAYS HAD BEGUN TO WARM and brighten, but the nights still followed with a hard chill. Connie and Joyce hung shivering a little in the shadows at one side of Texaco Jack's station. Their breaths misted in the air.

The station was closed, had been for a couple of hours. Connie and Joyce had arrived a quarter-hour ago. They'd asked a few indirect questions about town, had been told the truck they were looking for was probably the one parked over at Texaco Jack's. Moments after they'd arrived, two cars full of kids had wheeled into the lot, and Connie and Joyce had gone scuttling to cover. They didn't know why. It was just the sense that there was something furtive about their hunt for Harold, and that they shouldn't be seen.

The kids in the cars had parked to discuss their options for the rest of the night. There was a party at someone's called Big Phil's, and another at Brenda's, and a third faction wanted to go to the Union Pizzaria.

One of the cars had a CB. Now and then it blurted out a message. The final one Joyce and Connie overheard before the kids left was one that cut to the quick of their own personal concern.

"Mercy sakes alive," said the sender. "This is the Priest telling you to put on a heart of mercy, kindness, humility, and patience. Bear with one another and forgive one another. Even as the Lord has forgiven you, so also do you forgive. Now is that a four?"

The kids left, leaving Joyce and Connie to reflect, unhappily, upon this message.

They walked around the station to Harold's big Kenworth.

"There it is," Connie said. "That's his."

Joyce looked at it as if it contained the lost days of her youth. "I've always loved that truck."

"It's just a truck. How can you love a truck?"

"Oh, it's not really the truck. It's more the memories. The morning after Harold would come home, the boys and I would take to washing it. 'Course the boys could only reach halfway up the wheels, so after they did the bottom part, we'd roll it back so they could get the top. Once Lucy, the cat, was snoozing behind the front tire. I never knew what flat really was until then."

"As a pancake?"

"Flatter. More like a crepe. A hairy crepe. The boys brought it to Show and Tell in a plastic bag."

"Well, we found it. What do you want to do?"

"With the truck?"

"Yeah."

"Blow it up," Joyce said. "I don't care."

Connie scratched her head. "How about if we let the load loose?"

"Fine with me."

They went around to the back of the trailer. Connie unlocked the rear gate. "Grab that end over there."

They shifted the wooden ramp into position, lowered the end to the ground, and opened the doors.

The cattle did not require prodding. They came charging out of the truck and down the ramp, clomping, snorting, shaking, and bellowing.

Connie and Joyce scurried out of the way to safety, and watched from a distance.

The cattle milled about, congregated briefly around the gas pumps, as if holding a caucus, then one, the largest, trotted out into the road, paused looking about, then bellowed and started off at a moderate clip into the night. The rest followed.

Connie smiled after them. Joyce smiled after them. Connie and Joyce smiled at each other.

In the morning, Texaco Jack, wearing high rubber boots, waded through mounds of still squishy cow manure with a grimace of rage on his face and a high-pressure water hose in his hands. He was trying to hose the stuff off his blacktop, but was managing mostly to scatter it about in explosive bursts, making it all the soggier and more difficult to deal with.

"I want him outta here!" he bellowed at Cochise, who stood scratching his head and looking in wonder. "I want him and his fucking truck outta here today. Look at this, will you! Just look at this!"

Cochise looked. "Sure is a lot of shit," he said.

Across town, an hour later, Joyce stood in Connie's room holding the curtains back from the window and peeking down at Hot Coffee's red Winnebago in the motel's parking lot.

"Read it again," she said.

Connie held a letter that had just been delivered by a bellhop.

" 'Dear Connie and Joyce,' " she read. " 'By now you must know. I'm not proud of what I've done, but I'm not sorry about it either. I still think you're two of the best women the good Lord ever put on this earth. And so whatever happens, I'll always love you and be proud to be your husbands. Maybe we should talk about this. I'm in the red camper out in the lot. P.S. That was a mean thing, letting my cattle loose like that. I suppose now we're even.' "

Joyce let the curtains fall. The two women looked at each other blankly.

"That's what I thought he said," Joyce said.

Harold sat across from Hot Coffee at the dinette in the Winnebago drumming his fingertips and glancing at his watch every few seconds.

"If they were going to come," he said anxiously, "they should have been here by now."

"Relax," Hot Coffee advised solicitously.

"Relax! My life's been dumped into a toilet bowl and my wife, er, my wives are about to pull the handle."

There was a knock at the door.

Harold sprang up, stood stock still, trembling,

then tried to compose himself and sauntered casually to answer it.

"Connie!" he said with a big smile. "Joyce! How about this?"

The women entered stiffly, without acknowledging his greeting.

Hot Coffee got up and moved back to the galley to give them all some semblance of privacy.

Connie shot her a sour glance. "Has she known about this?"

"I knew he was married," Hot Coffee said brightly. "I just didn't know how married."

Harold swept his hand toward the dinette. "Come on," he said, voice filled with bonhomie. "Sit down, sit down."

Joyce and Connie seated themselves on one side. Harold sat down across from them, bobbing his head and grinning to let them know how happy he was to see them.

They stared back woodenly.

"How're the kids?" Harold asked, for lack of any better idea.

Joyce broke into tears.

"That wasn't the best thing to say, Harold," Connie said. "Not by a long shot."

"Sorry." Harold handed Joyce a handkerchief. "Here."

From the galley, Hot Coffee said, "Before we start, would anyone like some coffee? I've just brewed some Vienna Roast."

"That would be fine," Connie said.

Composed again, Joyce answered, "Yes, please."

"Coffee all around," Harold said, as if he were buying for the bar. He looked back to his wives, folded his hands before him, paused a moment, then said, "Now the way I see things is like this.

We've got a problem. I'm not going to beat around the bush. We've got a problem. Basically I think we've got a communications problem."

Joyce and Connie looked at each other.

"What the hell . . ." Connie said.

". . . is this man talking about?" Joyce finished.

The Nazi and his guns had shaken Cochise's spirit. He couldn't bring himself to go out after maverick CB-ers again. Spider didn't blame him. He'd been pretty frazzled by it himself. But he was still determined. He was out in the Nomad alone, working the loop antenna, and zeroing in, he was pretty sure, on the Priest.

". . . and that's what it says in Ephesians, friends. And that's the Gospel, you'd better believe it."

Spider keyed his mike. "Breaker, breaker. Do I have the Priest?"

"You got The Priest. Go."

"How about giving me your call letters, Priest?"

"Ten-four, Spider. It is you, isn't it, Spider? That's G-O-D."

"Very funny, Priest. How about a license? You got one of those?"

"I've got more than a license. I've got The Word."

"That's nice, Priest, but you're in violation of FCC regulations. You're also pushing illegal power."

"The power of the Lord knows no bounds. Do you believe in G-O-D, Spider?"

"Maybe yes, maybe no—what's that got to do with anything?"

"Because," the Priest replied with triumph, "I don't believe in the FCC."

"Clever," Spider said. "Clever." He was working the loop, studying the map clipped to the dash.

"Let me ask you something," the Priest said.

"Go ahead."

"Who gave us the airwaves in the first place?"

"I give up."

"Isn't He entitled to at least one channel?"

"Hey, who are you anyway?"

"The Priest," the Priest said somberly.

"I know your handle. And we know that mine's Spider. But that doesn't mean I'm a spider, does it? For Christ's sake, you're not talking to a spider, you're talking to a man."

"Very good—as far as it goes. But it's all the same in the eye of the Lord. Spider, man, hirsute, pinhead. . . ."

"Give me a break, will ya?" Spider said, taking a hard right, checking the reading from the loop and slowing down. "Give me a break."

"As you request—we gone!"

Spider looked out the side window. He didn't believe it. He was in front of the massive graystone visage of St. Leo's Church. He checked the map again. There wasn't any mistake.

He shook his head, sighed, and got out of the car and walked up the steps, through the tall wooden doors.

A timbered, vaulted ceiling soared above him. The air was close and still. A vigil light burned before the ornate marble altar. The church was empty save for two old people earnestly murmuring the rosary in a rear pew and a pious-looking woman dusting the statues.

Spider walked down the long aisle to the altar, eyes flicking from side to side like a TV detective's. He didn't see anything. He knelt, tried to think of a prayer, but couldn't—eyes still roaming—so feeling a little guilty, he got up and started to retrace his steps toward the rear.

A confessional door opened and a man stepped out with downcast eyes and a morose expression, slipped into a pew and bowed his head, fervently began his penance.

Spider hesitated, then turned toward the confessional. He closed the door behind him, confining himself in the dark small space, knelt, and waited.

A small panel slid open before his face, the silhouette of the confessor dimly visible behind the close mesh screen.

"Yes?" said a deep, sonorous, comforting voice.

Spider furrowed his brow, concentrating. Was it the same voice?"

"Yes?"

It was hard to tell. "Uh," he said, trying to remember how to do it. His mother had been a nut for the church and the whole family had attended mass as scrupulously as a diabetic administered insulin shots to himself, but after she died they didn't bother much, and he couldn't even remember the last time he'd been in a confessional. "Uh, bless me Father for I have sinned," he said, and then went silent, unhappy because there was something else he was supposed to say but he couldn't remember what.

The confessor waited, then prompted. "How long has it been since your last confession, my son?"

That was it. Sure. He cursed himself for being a dummy. "Uh, let me see, it was, yeah, it must be about nineteen years."

"Nineteen years!" the confessor said, losing his poise for a moment. "That *is* a long time."

"Yes, Father," Spider answered, feeling a little chastened.

The confessor regained his sanctified detachment. "And what are your sins, my son?"

Memories surged up within Spider, and he felt again the comfort, the relief he'd experienced in his childhood, the sense that he was not an evil person, that God understood all and would forgive.

"Well," he said, struggling to find the way to phrase it, the thing that had been bothering him more and more. "I've had bad thoughts about my father."

"What kind of thoughts?"

"Oh, I don't know. Just bad thoughts."

"Do you wish him harm?"

"No." Spider was somewhat annoyed. If the priest had known his father, that question would have been rhetorical. "I want to kill him sometimes, that's all."

"I see. In other words, you've sinned against the third commandment. You must fight against these thoughts."

Oh, that's just fine, Spider thought. That's a lot of help. "Yes, Father," he said.

"Have you other sins to confess?"

This wasn't doing any good at all. "No, Father," he said curtly.

"In nineteen years?"

"No."

"Are you married?"

"Uh-uh."

"You're a young man. . . . You're sure you have nothing else to confess?"

"No, I don't."

"Hard to believe." The priest paused. "Well, then, say ten Hail Marys, ten Our Fathers, and make a good Act of Contrition."

"Oh, my God, I am heartily sorry," Spider said, his mind racing ahead, trying to remember the words, "for having offended thee . . . uh . . . and I firmly resolve to . . . uh . . . sin no more."

"That's a big roger ten-four, Spider, fer sure!" the priest boomed. "We gone!"

The door to the priest's cubicle opened and slammed.

Spider shot to his feet, banging his head. He reeled back against the wall, caught his balance, shook his head, jerked open the door, and rushed outside.

The priest was gone. He whipped his gaze all about the church. But the priest—the Priest— was gone. He shook his head in disbelief. It was nearly a miracle. Of sorts.

Connie and Joyce both looked drawn. There was strain in Harold's face. Hot Coffee was as merry and bubbly as ever. They were taking a respite from their encounter. Harold was at the door of the Winnebago paying the delivery boy for the two pies—mushrooms, sausage, onions, and pep- eroni, hold the anchovies—they'd ordered from Mr. Pizza.

"This is very good coffee," Joyce said to Hot Coffee. "May I have another cup please?"

Hot Coffee sprang up with a cheery "Sure!" She took great pride in her hot coffee, literal as well as metaphorical, and she always responded well to people who appreciated her efforts as much as she did herself.

"Where's the washroom?" Connie asked.

Standing at the galley, Hot Coffee nodded. "That door over there."

"Thank you."

Harold brought the cardboard boxes to the table. "Pizza."

Hot Coffee put plates down. Harold placed a slice on each. He bit into his, used his finger to hook up the long string of gooey cheese that drooped down over his chin.

"Where were we?" he asked.

"You said we have to be open and trust our feelings," Joyce said. "I asked how. You said you didn't know."

"That's right." Harold nodded sagely.

"Then you said we have to think about what's best for the kids. I asked what's that. You said you didn't know."

"We have to be patient with ourselves," Harold counseled.

From the bathroom came an ear-splitting: "Aiiii!"

Harold jumped to his feet. "Connie?"

Joyce stood too. "Connie, what's wrong?"

The door opened a moment later. Connie emerged, casting an uncertain glance back over her shoulder.

"That damn toilet shot cold water at me," she said shakily.

"I'm sorry." Hot Coffee said. "You must've sat on the bidet."

"I don't care what it is, you better get that thing fixed before somebody gets hurt."

Connie sat down and picked up her pizza. They ate in silence several moments, casting covert glances at one another.

"Listen," Hot Coffee said. "I don't want to butt in on anyone else's business or anything, but after listening to all this talk about breaking up and who gets what and so on, I'd like to say something. Does anyone mind?"

Connie shrugged.

"Well," Joyce said, looking from her to Harold and back, "you seem to be a part already, so I guess you might as well."

"I wish *somebody* could come up with something," Harold said.

"Okay. It's like this. I figure you all wouldn't be here talking like this if you didn't still care about each other in the first place. And in the short time since you've met, you girls seem to have taken a liking to each other. Right?"

Connie and Joyce verified this with shy smiles.

"Good. So why not talk about staying together? I don't mean in the same house or anything. But a duplex doesn't seem like a bad idea." Hot Coffee beamed her widest smile around the table.

"A duplex?" Connie asked sourly.

"No," said Joyce.

"It's out of the question," Connie said.

"No way," Joyce reaffirmed.

"Absolutely not," Connie insisted.

Harold looked enchanted with the idea.

CHAPTER 14

It was an hour past nightfall. Spider was on the road. The talk coming through his radio was all in accordance with regulations. Maybe his crusade was having some effect.

"Lookin' for that Spider," came a harsh, familiar voice. "You out there tonight?"

Spider picked up his mike. "This here's Spider. Go ahead."

"You got a gun, Spider?"

"Who's this? Blood?"

"We got guns, lots of 'em. All sizes."

"I'm glad for you, Blood." Spider started turning the loop antenna on the roof.

"They make all kinds of nasty holes. Big ones, small ones. You name it."

"Hey, Blood, sorry but I don't take anonymous threats."

"We know who you are and where you are."

"You want to make a threat," Spider said hotly, "then make it to my face."

"And we know how to get you. . . ." Blood said.

Harold, weary, beaten down, sat at the dinette with his head in his hands staring vacantly at the Formica. Hot Coffee was in a chair in the galley, patiently working on some intricate needlepoint.

Connie and Joyce were in the living room, huddled together in murmured conversation. They went silent after some time, then rose together and returned to the table.

"Okay," Connie said. "This is what we'll do. We'll try it, but only on a thirty-day trial basis. If it doesn't work out, that's it."

Relief flooded Harold's face. "Okay," he said quickly. Then he wrinkled his brow. "Where?"

"What's wrong with Dallas?" Connie asked.

Joyce shook her head. "I don't feel right about Dallas. Not since sixty-three."

"That's silly," Connie said.

"I just don't feel right about it."

"What about Union?" Hot Coffee suggested. "It's nice here. No one's ever bothered me."

Joyce shook her head. "We'd have to yank all the kids out of school."

"Portland?" Harold offered.

Joyce looked amenable. Connie shrugged. She was a master of the shrug. It was her most eloquent means of expression. She could convey more with one shrug than most people could with an hour's worth of yammering. This one said, *What the hell? It's no crazier than any of the rest.*

"All right," Joyce said. "But just a thirty-day trial, remember."

"Right," said Connie.

"We're agreed, then," Harold said. He sighed mightily.

They stood up.

"I think we could all use some sleep," Harold said.

Joyce asked, "Debbie, can I help you with the dishes?"

"No, it's nothing."

Connie shook Hot Coffee's hand. "Thanks for everything."

"We'll come to say goodbye before we leave," Harold said.

Hot Coffee saw them to the door, stood in it a moment watching them walk back toward the motel.

Harold put a husbandly arm around each of his wives.

Hot Coffee smiled. She liked stories that had a happy ending.

Spider drove with compressed lips and a cold anger growing in the pit of his stomach.

"It's all over, Spider," Blood said. "All over."

Spider took a right off a commercial street onto a tree-lined residential one.

"Blood. . . ."

"I'd leave Union if I were you."

Spider turned the antenna, took a new reading, circled a four-block area on his map.

"Blood. . . ."

"Better yet, leave the state." In the background was the sound of a TV game show.

"Blood, I'm having trouble copying you. Try turning down the TV."

There was silence.

"Blood."

He wasn't answered.

"Blood, you still there? Come on."

Nothing.

"Damn! You got a copy, Blood?"

Static.

He hung a left.

Blood returned, faint at first, then growing stronger. "You think you're hot stuff, doncha, Spider?"

Spider worked the antenna.

"Lemme tell you something," Blood continued. "You ain't shit."

"What am I?"

"You ain't shit. How 'bout that? We gonna tear you apart piece by piece and enjoy the whole show."

Blood's voice faded to static.

"Break to the River Rat," said a faint new voice.

"Go break."

Spider pulled to the curb and sat listening to the new voices in frustration.

"Lemme tell you something." Blood's voice sounded again as the intruders faded out. "You've been interfering in people's lives and a lot of people don't like it."

Spider burned rubber swinging back into traffic.

"What people, Blood? Mind being more specific?"

Spider studied his readings as Blood spoke and turned yet again.

"You've been sticking your nose where it doesn't belong. Now you're gonna get it chopped off. My advice to you is—get out of Union. 'Cause one way or another you're not gonna be around for long. Now you can take my advice. Or you can leave it. That's your business. I couldn't care less."

There was interference.

"Blood—"

Static.

"Come on back, Blood. . . ."

But Spider didn't need the voice anymore. He was abreast of a squat brick apartment building. He eased over to the curb, sat looking at the building a moment in reluctant suspicion, then checked the figures he'd jotted down while taking his fixes.

Slowly, and unhappily, he got out of Nomad.

He went into the building and rode the elevator up to the third floor, walked part way down the hall, stopped and knocked on a door.

"It's open," said a voice from within.

Spider entered into a darkened, but familiar living room. A TV was on in the corner, a game show droning at low volume.

Dean was slouched in a Naugahyde chair next to a coffee table on which stood an open half-empty bottle of Old Crow and a CB transceiver. He looked at Spider with dull, hurt eyes.

"What is this, Dean?" Spider said softly.

Dean raised and lowered his eyebrows, as if to say, Who knows, who cares?

"What is this?" Spider repeated, his voice growing louder. "I want to know. You can't face your own brother? I'll tell you what this is. This is horseshit." He paused, waiting for a response that didn't come. "This is horseshit and you know it!"

Dean turned his head languidly toward the television.

"You know it, don't you?" Spider said, feeling

his face flush. "Look, you can't even face me now. You can't even look at me." He crossed to stand in front of his brother. "Dean? Dean? *Stand up, goddamnit, and face me for once!* It's me, Blaine, your brother! We grew up together, remember? *Goddamnit, look at me!*"

He made a sudden grab for Dean't shirt and pulled him up to his feet.

"You want to tell me something, you tell me to my face. You want to tell me to go fuck myself, you tell me. But no horseshit, Dean. No horseshit threats over the radio. You want to take a shot at me, you take a shot at me. I'm your brother. That's what I'm here for. Go ahead. Go ahead, goddamnit!"

Dean's face was sullen and numbly embarrassed.

"*Go ahead!*" Spider shouted.

He slapped Dean, who did nothing.

"*Go ahead!*"

He slapped him a second time. This time Dean jerked away and hit Spider a clumsy blow to the mouth.

Spider stood still. A trickle of blood appeared on his lip, but he made no move to wipe it away.

"Okay," he said quietly. "I'm your brother. I still love you. Nothing can change that. That's what I'm here for."

Dean broke into tears. He threw his arms around Spider and buried his face against Spider's shoulder.

Spider held him tightly. They stood motionless in each other's arms.

"Now we can talk. . . ." Spider whispered.

CHAPTER 15

RICHIE WEBBER GUIDED HIS FATHER'S OLDSMObile past the parked cars in the moonlit lover's lane with the lights out, looking for a space.

He found one, killed the engine, and lit and smoked a cigarette to calm his nerves before he turned on the CB. He adjusted the channel selector and keyed the mike.

"Lookin' for that Electra," he said. "Lookin' for that Electra one time. Come on. . . ."

A little across town, Pam was sitting at her kitchen table drinking a cup of coffee and working up a lesson plan for the next day. She heard her call name over her CB in the bedroom.

She went in. "Electra here," she said to the mike. "Is this the Warlock?"

"Ten-four, Electra."

"How've you been?"

"Sorta down. I've been going through some heavy things."

"Me too, Warlock. Maybe we can help each other." Pam sat down on the bed, stretched out, and made herself comfortable. "Can we loosen a few buttons?"

"Uh, okay. What do you have on?"

"What do you think?"

"Transparent something?"

"No. Guess again."

"A towel?"

"No."

"I give up."

"All I have on is . . . my radio."

Spider left Dean's apartment in a state of quiet misery. He drove over to Pam's house with neither the CB nor the tape player on. He drove in blunted silence, alone with his thoughts.

Pam's car was at the curb and the lights were on, but she didn't answer his knock. He tried again, touched the doorknob. It was unlocked. He cracked the door and stuck his head in.

"Pam?" he called.

He walked in. "Pam?"

She wasn't in the living room, or the kitchen. Standing in the kitchen doorway, he heard her voice, faintly, from the bedroom, and an answering voice from her CB. He went down the hall.

Pam held the mike close to her lips. "Oh, Warlock. . . ." she breathed.

Richie's voice was tinged with urgency. "Keep going, keep going!"

"Oh, yes, yes. . . ." Pam said.

"Keep going," Richie moaned.

There was a tap on the door, which made Pam jump.

"Pam?"

"Blaine?" she said incredulously.

"Yeah." He opened the door and came in.

"Uh, stand by Warlock," she said.

"*Stand by?*" came the anguished voice from the radio.

"Better finish your call," Blaine said.

"What do you want?" she asked, flustered. She added, into the mike, "Warlock, I'm still here."

"Please don't stop," Richie begged.

"What do you want?" Pam asked Spider. "Hurry."

"Electra!" Richie wailed. "Come back!"

"What do you want!" Pam demanded of Blaine.

"The cake," Spider said, frowning. "I want the cake. Electra?"

"Stand by, Warlock."

"No!" Richie cried.

"Electra," Spider said, mouth turning down at the corners.

"Please, Blaine—" Pam said. "Warlock, hang on a sec—"

"Nooo! Not now!"

Spider's voice went hard. "Where's the cake, Electra? You were supposed to pick up the cake."

"Blaine, please, just a minute. . . ."

"In the fridge?"

"Yes."

"Help!" Richie called.

"Take all the time you want—*Electra.*" Spider turned and stalked out.

"Blaine, damn you—" She said to the mike, "Warlock, stand by, please, don't hate me—"

"Nooo!"

In the kitchen, Spider yanked open the refrigerator. A big watermelon blocked his view of the back shelves. He hoisted it out, cradled it in one arm, and pushed aside the cans and packages with his free hand, searching for the cake. He couldn't find it. He returned the watermelon and slammed the door. It bounced back off the melon. He shoved the melon farther in and tried again, but the door still wouldn't close. He tried a third time, angry. The bulky melon refused to allow the latch to catch. He lost control and attacked the door with a flurry of kicks and punches. The seizure lasted several moments, winding and exhausting him, but when it was done the door was closed. He stood breathing heavily and trembling a little. He turned.

Pam was leaning against the kitchen counter watching him. They stared at each other in long uncomfortable silence.

"The cake's behind you," Pam said finally.

Spider glanced over his shoulder and saw the cake box on the kitchen table. He returned his eyes to Pam's.

His shoulders slumped. "Why did you do it?" he said quietly.

"Do what?"

"You know what."

"Well, you rescue people your way—Electra rescues people her way. How's that?"

Spider shook his head. "I don't mean that."

"What do you mean?"

"I mean Blood."

"Blood?"

"Yeah."

"What's that?"

Spider exploded. "That's what you sleep with! That's what you're taking to Baltimore!"

"You're crazy."

"I'm not crazy! Everybody's someone else around here! I'm not crazy!" He stalked around the room in circles, pounding his fist into his hand. Then he stopped and forced himself to breathe quietly a moment. "What about it?" he said.

"What about what?"

"Baltimore."

"You mean Dean?"

Spider stiffened at the name.

"That was just talk," Pam said.

"He said it was more than talk."

"I was his friend."

"He said you were more than a friend."

"We were good friends but, my God, he was straighter than you. I didn't think anyone could be straighter than you."

"So you didn't mean it, about Baltimore."

"Yes. No. I don't know."

"But you don't mean it now."

Pam hesitated. Then she said, "No."

"You're gonna hurt him. . . . Why'd you do it?"

"Because you weren't here!" she said hotly. "Because I lost out to a batch of transistors. Because while you were out saving lives and playing FBI—"

"FCC," Spider corrected.

"While you were out doing that, I was sitting around with a goddamned radio in my bed! Because you were married to your father, that's why! *Because you weren't here, you lunkhead.* Because if you were, we'd be here sipping coffee knowing how much we love each other!"

Tears were running freely down her cheeks. She rushed out of the room and down the hall.

Spider looked down at his hands. "This is all very discouraging," he said to himself. "I think I'll go. . . ."

He picked up the cake, walked from the kitchen through the front door, and left.

When he started the Nomad, Pam's bedroom window flew open. She stuck her head out and shouted, "Go bust a few old ladies, sheriff! It'll probably make you feel better!"

He pulled away from the curb, thinking about what she'd said. After a few blocks, he turned abruptly, and drove north a little ways, parked in front of the house of the little old lady in the wheelchair. He took a roll of electrician's tape from the glove compartment, got out, snuck around the back, and spliced together the antenna wire he'd cut.

Back in the Nomad, he turned on his CB, moved the channel selector, and heard the happy droning voice: "So when Marnie was about twelve, this boy next door gave her a big red rose. Why Tom and I—"

Spider smiled, turned the set off, and drove home.

At the Funny Farm, he found his father conked out with booze again, slumped over the table. Even Ned the Dog had failed him. Ned had gone to sleep in the middle of eating, was collapsed on his side with his head part way into his food bowl, snoring loudly.

Spider sighed. He took down a couple of plates

and opened the cake box. He looked at the cake and said, "That figures."

It bore only slight resemblance to the one he'd ordered. The chocolate frosting was embroidered with sugar roses. HAPPY BIRTHDAY, DAD, it read. There wasn't a truck or a highway in sight.

Spider rummaged through drawers until he found a box of candles he remembered seeing. He stuck them in the cake, brought it over to the table with the plates.

He put a hand on his father's shoulder and shook it gently. "Pop. Pop. How 'bout some cake, Pop?"

Floyd wouldn't wake up.

Spider went out to his workshop. He turned on his transceiver and keyed the mike. "How 'bout it, Papa Thermodyne? You got your ears on tonight? Come on!"

He waited. After a moment, he heard a mike keyed in response, some shuffling, noisy throat clearing, then a blurry voice: "Mercy, this here's that one Papa Thermodyne and we got one helluva copy, so mercy, come on— What's the handle?"

Spider turned off the set and went back into the house.

"Your son Blaine is the handle," he said. Then he sang, "Happy birthday to you. Happy Birthday to you. Happy Birthday dear Pop. Happy Birthday to you."

Floyd looked at him as if he'd just done something disappointing and treacherous. "Okay. . . ."

Spider lit the candles and placed the cake on the table between them.

"Pop," he said, trying for a hearty tone, "I know you would o' liked it if we had some more of the crew here, but Roy's in Alaska and Donny's still in the slammer and Dean really wanted to come, but he was feeling a little under the weather. So I guess it'll just be us, but that's good because it'll give us a chance to talk a little before I leave—"

Floyd's face brightened at the mention of the word *leave*.

Two candles flickered out.

"Now don't get nervous," Spider said in quick reassurance. "I'll make sure you won't go without anything. I'll make sure of that. But the thing is, it's high time I get out and do something with my life and maybe when I do you'll like me all the better for it. Now I know I haven't always been all the things to you that you wanted me to be. I know that and I'm sorry for all the times I've fallen short in your eyes."

Two more candles sputtered and died.

"Then again," Spider said, "you haven't exactly been a barrel of monkeys yourself. But we toughed it out and hung together and I guess that's how it is with two people as close as us."

A fifth candle died.

"But what I really want to say is I don't know where I'll be or what I'll be doing, but whatever it is—" Spider faltered, his voice filled with emotion. "Wherever it is, I'll always be proud to be your son. And . . . if anyone ever says bad things about you, if someone says, 'That Floyd Lovejoy is a so-and-so,' I'll fight 'em, I will . . . because . . . well . . . that's the way I feel." He nodded at the cake, voice firming again. "There's only a couple of candles left, so maybe you better make a wish and blow 'em out. Are you making a wish? Want me to help blow 'em out? All right."

Spider blew out the last two candles.

"I hope your wish comes true," he said.

Floyd nodded impassively. "Okay. . . ."

CHAPTER 16

PAM ARRIVED AT THE FUNNY FARM EARLY THE next morning. She had spent a sleepless unhappy night, rolling in her tangled sheets, unable to find any relief but short fitful dozings, from which she wakened abruptly with small cries.

She had to see Blaine.

The gray April sky was pouring rain down in torrents, against which the windshield wipers were nearly useless. Water blew in past the weather seal on her door, soaking the edge of the seat, and dripped from the air vent onto her leg. It was a thoroughly miserable day, an unfortunately perfect mirror for the state of her own emotions.

She parked next to Spider's workshop and waited in her car, hoping for a break in the lashing sheets of rain. None came. She gritted her teeth, jumped out and popped open her umbrella, and ran for the house. Her back and the legs of her slacks got soaked by the short sprint.

She pushed open the kitchen door and jumped through it into shelter without knocking.

Dean was sitting at the table sipping from a mug of coffee.

She was startled. "Dean—"

Dean was equally surprised. "Pam. Hello."

Ned the Dog looked up from his bowl, where he was gustily having at the leftover portion of Floyd's birthday cake, which was everything but a small slice. He gave Pam a single cursory wag of his tail, then went back to work.

"Where's Blaine?" Pam asked, uncomfortable in Dean's presence.

"Well, we've got a little problem here." Dean paused, looked out the window to the driving rain, then said, "Pop disappeared in the middle of the night."

Before he could get any further, Blaine came in from the workshop in boots and a poncho, carrying a bullhorn wrapped in a big plastic bag. His face was tense and troubled. He nodded a small greeting to Pam.

"We ought to get moving," he said. "We'll talk in the car."

The Nomad's windshield wipers whipped furiously back and forth, but still visibility was difficult through the driving rain. Dean was behind the wheel, Spider on the other side, and Pam wedged between them.

A voice from the CB said, "I heard he was dead. What did you hear?"

"I don't know," another voice answered. "I just heard it over Seven."

"Did you get Cal?" Spider asked Dean.

"Yeah, but he said he wanted to work Nine and Fifteen a little more before coming over."

Someone from the CB said, "I'm heading out as soon as I finish these pancakes."

"Where're you setting up?" Spider asked.

"Where the fire road starts."

"Good."

"Call Leprechaun," said the CB. "He needs a ride up there."

"How do you know where to look?" Pam asked.

"Dean found some tracks," Spider said. He paused a moment, then said, "Right here," as Dean pulled over to the side, abreast of a dense woods.

Spider hefted the plastic bag. "Well . . ."

He and Dean reached across Pam and clasped each other's hand strongly. Then Spider pushed open the door, got out, and plunged into the woods.

Dean put the Nomad in gear. Pam followed Spider's diminishing figure with her eyes. This did not escape Dean.

"If only," he said, "I didn't have track this spring."

Pam offered him a faint, bittersweet smile.

"I hate track," Dean said.

The storm had turned the woods into something nightmarishly primeval—dark, wind-lashed, angry, and threatening. The wind howled, rain beat down in whips, branches slashed about. It was hard to see.

Spider was stumbling through the forest carrying a bullhorn wrapped in a protective plastic bag. He was wearing a poncho but the wind drove rain in at the wrists and the sides of the hood, and soaked his lower pantlegs. His lips were blue with cold and his hands beefy and raw.

He came upon a small clearing, stood under the ineffectual shelter of a big pine, and removed the bullhorn from its cover. He put it to his mouth.

"Lookin' for that Floyd!" he called, the amplified voice dulled and muted by the storm. *"Lookin' for that Floyd! You got a copy?"*

He listened. He heard nothing but the whistle of the wind. He covered the bullhorn, hunched his neck into his shoulders, lowered his head, and trudged forward again.

Dean had broadcast calls for help shortly after arriving at the Funny Farm. The responses were quick and unanimously sympathetic. It was agreed that everyone would meet at the fire road in an hour.

Dean and Pam got there early, but almost everyone was there already, and the rest arrived within the next fifteen minutes. In addition to guys on foot with bullhorns and walkie-talkies, there was a large assemblage of pickup trucks, cars, and vans, and even one behemoth of a Kenworth eighteen-wheeler.

Hunched up against the rain, Dean went to the first vehicle in the line, Texaco Jack's big GMC wrecker. The bearded man rolled down his window.

Dean shouted in to him, "Take it east on the frontage road. We're monitoring Twelve."

Jack nodded, cranked up his window, shifted into gear, and moved out.

The Kenworth rolled up to the lead position. There were two women in the high cab next to the driver—a blonde and a brunette, both pretty. There was a name stenciled on the door—Harold Rissley, the Chrome Angel.

"Any luck?" the driver asked.

"Not yet."

"Well, we'd like to help."

"Thanks very much," Dean said, genuinely touched. "Your rig's pretty big for the frontage road. Take it up around that corner ahead, then hang a left and follow the intersecting road east. It loops around the forest and comes back. We're monitoring Twelve."

The driver nodded.

The brunette leaned across him and called down, "Could you tell me, please—has anyone reported seeing any lost cattle?"

"Not that I know of."

The brunette looked disappointed, and for some reason, a little guilty.

"What's the name of the guy we're lookin' for again?" the driver asked.

"Floyd."

The driver made a thumbs up sign, rolled his window closed, and moved the Kenworth off.

An open-top Jeep pulled up next, driven by a boy of enormous bulk covered by a yellow rain slicker.

"Hey, Cochise!" Dean said.

There was a creek in Spider's path, swollen to flood level by the downpour, the water muddy and frothy. Spider walked right into it without hesitation, wading thigh-deep to the other side. He couldn't get any wetter or colder than he already was.

At the top of the other bank, he unlimbered the bullhorn again.

"Floyd Lovejoy! How abou—" the horn snapped and crackled as the wind drove a sheet of rain against it, and then died. Spider fiddled with it, but it was short-circuited and useless. He dropped it back into the bag and called with his own voice. It was doubtful whether his words carried more than a few yards.

He walked ahead a little to the stump of a fallen tree and climbed up on it to look around. He shielded his eyes with a hand and turned a full 360 degrees. Nothing. He was about to jump down, when he caught a vague motion in the corner of his vision.

He squinted. Yes! The shadowy outline of a man, moving slowly away from him.

He leapt down and took off at a dead run, boots splattering in the sodden earth.

"Pop! Pop!"

The figure continued its retreat.

"Pop!" Spider shouted.

He fell, rolled through a puddle, was up and running again, closing the gap.

"Pop!" he screamed, only a few yards separating them now.

The figure stopped and turned. Spider came up short, then took a step backward. He was looking into the surly, rain-wet face of the Nazi.

"Are you Floyd?" the Nazi growled. He didn't recognize Spider at all.

"Uh, no," Spider said.

The Nazi shook a fist at the trees around him. "How the hell do they expect us to find the pea-picker if we don't even know what he looks like!"

He turned and shuffled off into the gloom, muttering to himself.

At the checkpoint, a black Dodge sedan pulled up beside Dean. The driver was in his late twenties, with long wavy hair and a friendly, good-humored face. Beneath his open windbreaker, Dean saw that he wore the white collar of a Catholic priest.

"Can you take Oak Hill road for us, Father?"

"Sure," the priest said.

"Great. We're monitoring Twelve."

The priest waved. "Keep the faith," he said, and drove off.

Next in line was a carful of students from the high school.

"You guys should be in class," Dean remonstrated gently. "But thanks for coming."

Les, Cal, and Tony, Spider's drinking buddies, were slogging through the woods with their hands cupped to their mouths, calling Floyd's name.

Les nudged Cal and pointed. Cal nudged Tony.

From out of a stand of brush had come Ned the Dog, gamboling along as if on some interior holiday that made the weather completely irrelevant. Now and then he turned his head skyward, seemed to calculate a moment, then jumped to catch a large raindrop in his jaws.

"That's Floyd's dog, isn't it?" Les asked.

"Sure acts like him," Cal said.

Les clapped his hands. "Come here, boy! Take us to Floyd! Take us to Floyd!"

"Go get Floyd," Cal urged.

The dog looked at them, brow furrowed in concentration, then flung himself down into the mud, rolled over, got up again and wagged his tail, waiting for their approval.

"Dumb sonofabitch, ain't he?" Les said.

"Go on," said Cal. "Go get Floyd."

Ned performed his mud roll once again.

"That's not how you do it," Tony advised his friends. "You have to get a piece of clothing so they can get the scent. That's how dogs work."

"Go get Floyd, boy!" Cal said stubbornly. "Where's Floyd?"

Ned dove to the mud, rolled a third time, and got up looking enormously pleased with his ability to follow orders so well.

Spider emerged from the woods along a stretch of the frontage road. He was soaked, winded, and shaking with cold. He eased himself down on the trunk of a fallen tree to catch his breath.

There was movement to his left. He looked, blinked, and looked again.

In a wheelchair pushed by a young man who looked to be her grandson was the old woman who had been telling her endless life story over the CB, the one whose antenna wire he had cut. She was swathed in wool blankets, protected from the rain by a massive umbrella lashed to the arm of her chair. She wore a wide-brimmed rubber hat and had a pair of binoculars looped around her neck, which she lifted to her eyes at intervals to scan the treeline.

She nodded brightly to Spider as she rolled past.

Moments later, from the opposite direction, a young long-haired man with a cleric's collar visible at the open throat of his windbreaker, came jogging up, the picture of grace and athletic accomplishment. He held a megaphone in his hand. Every fourth step he lifted it and shouted through it: "Floyd! Floyd!"

He saluted Spider as he jogged past. "Couldn't see much out of the car. Thought I'd park and run it. Keep the faith."

He jogged out of sight.

Spider shook his head to clear it—either he was exhausted to the point of hallucinating, or the bloody woods were full of lunatics.

Hot Coffee's Winnebago was parked at the checkpoint. She had the heat turned up inside and was serving styrofoam cups of coffee and sandwiches to wet and tired searchers who came in to take a break.

A handful of them were clustered around the dinette, toweling off their wet hair and chafing their cold hands.

One, in steamy glasses, asked, "Anyone ever been an S & R before?"

"What's an S & R?" asked a man in dripping red mackinaw.

"Search and Rescue."

They looked at each other, shaking their heads no.

"This is my third one," said the man in the fogged glasses. "They're a lot of fun. You meet some real nice people."

The man in the mackinaw nodded agreeably.

"Damn, this coffee's good!" said a third man.

Hot Coffee smiled widely. "That's because I grind my own. It's better without styrofoam, but I ran short of cups on account of the emergency."

Cal, Les, and Tony stood under the pelting rain

staring at Ned the Dog, who was happily devouring the old sock of Floyd's that Tony was holding out to him.

"Tell me again how dogs work," Cal said.

"That's the dumbest goddamn dog I ever seen," Les said.

Tony dropped the end of the sock and shook his head. Ned swallowed the rest of the sock and belched. He looked up at them, eagerly waiting their next instructions.

"I mean," said Les, "he's even dumb for a dog. They ain't all like this. I had one once—he weren't smart exactly, but he weren't like this."

"Take us to Floyd, boy!" Cal said. "Go get Floyd!"

Ned promptly hit the mud again.

"He's just old," Tony said. "Maybe he's getting his signals crossed."

"Go get Floyd!" Cal ordered.

Ned flopped into the mud.

Tony scratched his head, staring at the dog. Suddenly he snapped his fingers. "Ned—roll over!"

Ned snapped to attention. His body stiffened. His tail went out rigid and straight. His ears rose up. He sniffed with machine gun-like rapidity and turned slowly forty-five degrees to the north.

He went "Aaaaaarroooooo!", then took off like a shot.

"Hot damn!" Tony said triumphantly.

Cal and Les exchanged glances, then they broke out after Tony, who was already after Ned.

There was a crackle from the walkie-talkie slung from Spider's shoulder beneath his poncho. He unzipped the poncho, pulled the walkie-talkie out, and pressed his ear to the little speaker.

"Mobile to Base," said Tony's voice. "Mobile to Base. I repeat: We've found Floyd. We've found Floyd. You'd better get up here."

"Ten-four roger, mobile unit," Dean's voice answered. "What's your twenty?"

"We're in a clearing about half-a-mile north of the old Farm Road."

"Is he all right? Is Floyd all right?"

"You'd better—" The rest was lost in static.

Spider jammed the walkie-talkie back and started running for the old Farm Road.

CHAPTER 17

SPIDER TRIPPED AND TUMBLED DOWN AN INCLINE as he approached the old Farm Road, bruising his leg on a rock. He splashed through ankle-deep pools of mud, leaped over fallen trees, tore his poncho, and cut his face smashing through underbrush.

At the edge of the forest, bordering the overgrown fields of a long-abandoned farm, Spider saw figures in various colored rain gear gathering. The blurred words of excited voices reached him, and the wild barking of Ned the Dog. He pushed himself the final distance, gasping for breath, pain knifing into his side.

He staggered to a halt, bracing an arm against a tree.

Bizarrely, the people around him were laughing. A big man in a hunting parka slapped his knee, guffawed, and pointed. Spider looked up, following the direction of the man's finger. His eyes widened and his jaw dropped.

Huddled close together in the center of the field were Harold Rissley's lost cows, cringing under the driving rain.

Floyd Lovejoy, in a drenched sheepskin coat and a cowboy hat, was astride one of them. He slapped the beast on the rump with his hat and dug his heels into its side.

"Yee-haa! Yee-haa!" he roared. "Git along little doggies!"

He was forcing the reluctant animal to circle and move the rest of the herd in a confused kind of roundup.

"Whoopee-tai-yai-aii, git along! Whaaa-haoo!"

Ned the Dog raced forward barking and nipped at the cows' heels to help Floyd.

"Go git 'em, Floyd!" one of the rescuers shouted.

"Ride 'em, cowboy!" another called.

The high school kids began a chorus of "Back in the Saddle Again."

Others joined them, and soon nearly everyone was singing:

"We're back in the saddle again,
"Out where a friend is a friend. . . ."

Spider watched in silence. A small smile came over his lips, a smile that was at once one of joy and sadness.

"Happy birthday, Pop," he whispered to himself.

A hand fell lightly on his shoulder. He turned. It was Pam, beneath her big black umbrella. They looked into each other's eyes a moment, then back at Floyd.

"Whoopie tiya yai," sang the rescuers,
"We're on our way,
"We're back in the saddle again. . . ."

Pam removed the ring box from her pocket and placed it in Spider's hand. He looked at it, closed his fingers about it, and sighed in resignation.

She smiled at him. "There are a lot of voices out there," she said, "but yours is different. I like what you said the best."

She lifted her left hand, extending her ring finger.

Three days had passed since the wild storm, which was dying winter's last bitter snarl, and Floyd's disappearance.

It was a bright, spring morning. In the storm's wake the sun had burned brilliantly, touched the grass with the first tinges of green, brought song to the throats of the returning birds, and coaxed the heads of flowers up from their beds.

On three separate roadways, three different cars were rolling along at moderate speeds toward a triple intersection a little out of town. The intersection was adjacent to a rolling field of spring flowers, backdropped by gentle greening hills.

In one car, a black Dodge, the Priest sat behind the wheel in formal black robes, his cassette player playing joyous organ music at high volume, his CB channel selector on Twelve, and his mike keyed open.

Approaching on the second road was Spider's Nomad, washed and waxed for the occasion. Spider and Dean, wearing their Sunday best, and carnations in their lapels, sat in the front seat listening to the booming organ music on Spider's

CB. Ned the Dog sat on the rear seat, his coat washed and brushed, barking happily at clouds and passing fence posts.

On the third road, Pam wheeled her white convertible with the top down, the sound of the wind mixing with the organ music, and flapping her white bridal gown and the gowns of Karen Dugan and the two other students from her gym class she'd asked to be her bridesmaids.

Nearing the intersection, the Priest punched the reject button on the tape player, killing the music, picked up his mike, crossed himself with it, and intoned, "In the name of the Father and of the Son and of the Holy Spirit. Come on—"

Approaching from the left, Spider crossed himself.

Approaching from the right, Pam did likewise.

Over the radio came a collective, "Amen."

Back at the Funny Farm, Floyd—not a bottle in sight, holding an uncharacteristic cup of black coffee—was gabbing excitedly into his CB with an old trucker who was passing somewhere nearby on the highway.

"Mercy that Canada's pretty country!" he said. "Doggone if it didn't rain most of the time we were at the ranch, but mercy sakes, I never saw such beauty in one place. Hey, good buddy, maybe someday we'll meet there and have a doggone good time, how 'bout that?"

Cochise, his enormity encased in a blue serge suit, stood in the center of the field that stretched out from the intersection, driving a stake into the ground. He attached an elastic cord to the stake, turned, and began walking toward the edge of the field, playing out cord from a reel as he went.

When he had fifty yards out, he stopped, hooked a small spring scale to it and tugged to check the tension. Satisfied, he returned the scale to his pocket, walked a few feet further to where he had set the huge model he'd finished the night before, then lifted it gently and carried it to the cord. The model was exquisite—intricately detailed, wingspan nearly fifteen feet, and lovingly painted with bright green acrylic. He cut the cord at the reel and attached the end of the piece that ran from the stake to the nose of his model. He rubbed his hands in pleasure, then looked up and down the roads leading to the intersection for the approach of the wedding party.

The Priest slowed for a blinking yellow light at a crossroads. Zooming through the crossroads ahead of him went a bright red Winnebago, closely pursued by an Oldsmobile driven by a young man.

The two vehicles were in brief communication over the channel the Priest's selector was set on.

"Hot Coffee," a boy's voice said, "you don't know me, but you were with my best friend last night—"

"What's the handle?" replied a friendly woman's voice.

"The Warlock."

"Well, mercy—come on, Warlock!"

The Winnebago and the Olds zipped around a curve and vanished from sight.

The Priest picked up his broadcast where he'd been interrupted.

"Now he enriches and strengthens you by a special sacrament so that you may assume the duties of marriage in mutual and lasting fidelity. Spider and Electra, have you come here freely and without reservation to give yourselves to each other in marriage?"

"I have," answered Spider over the radio.

"I have," said Pam.

"Will you love and honor each other as man and wife for the rest of your lives? Is that a four?"

"That's a four," Pam said.

"Big roger four," said Spider.

The Priest said, "Since it is your intention. . . ."

Another voice bled into the channel: "Withdrawing my tumescent member, I gazed at her thin body marked by thick purple welts like so many ropes, spanning the shoulders, the back, the buttocks, the belly and breasts, welts which sometimes overlapped and crisscrossed—"

"Breaker! Breaker!" radioed Spider.

"Here and there a little blood still oozed. 'Oh, how I love you,' she moaned."

"Breaker! Breaker!"

"Go breaker," said the voice.

"Yeah, uh, Triple-X," Spider said, "we're trying to have a little wedding here on Twelve and you're walking all over us."

"By golly, I'm definitely sorry about that. Terrible thing, terrible thing. Hey, is that Spider and Electra there?"

"Ten-four," Spider said.

"Hey, I heard about you two. Let me unload a bucketful of those good numbers on ya. This here's Triple-X wishin' you a good one. We're takin' it to Seven."

"Ahem, ahem," said the Priest. "Do you, Electra, take Spider to be your husband, to be true to him in good times and bad, in sickness and health, and to love him and honor him all the days of your life?"

"I do."

"And do you, Spider, take Electra as your wife, to be true to her in good times and bad, in sickness and in health, and to love her and honor her all the days of your life?"

"I do."

"Then I pronounce you man and wife. May the Lord in his goodness strengthen your consent and fill you both with his blessing. What God has joined, men must not divide. Now is that a four?"

The three cars converged on the intersection and came in sight of each other at the same time.

"That's a four," Pam said.

"You got the biggest four ever," said Spider.

The Priest pulled to a stop. The Nomad rolled up behind him. And Pam's convertible braked behind the Nomad. Everyone emerged grinning.

Spider grabbed Pam in his arms and swept her off her feet, kissed her long and hard. There were hugs all around, kisses, pats on the back. Ned the Dog dashed about, barking idiotically.

Dean approached Pam, hesitated over kissing her, then broke into a big smile, grabbed her, and planted one enthusiastically on her lips.

He grabbed Spider, hugged them both at once, and then they stood together posing for Karen's Instamatic.

A big Kenworth eighteen-wheeler came tooling down the road. Riding tall behind the wheel was

Harold, the Chrome Angel, and beside him was a pretty blonde, and beside her a pretty brunette. All three of them beamed at the wedding party. Harold gave them three quick blasts of his air-horn, and then the Kenworth was roaring away in the general direction of Des Moines.

"We're off!" Cochise called.

The sharp staccato of his model's engine sounded, the plane moved forward under the direction of the control box in his hands, then gained the air and soared upward. Unfurling behind it was a red velvet banner with the words, HAPPY WEDDING, SPIDER AND ELECTRA. Pam squealed in delight. The rest of the party cheered and clapped their hands.

The plane swooped low over them, Cochise working the controls, then circled, climbed high, came around, and dove for another pass.

It was greeted with cheers. Cochise beamed proudly.

Cochise sent the craft climbing again, but it was a little sluggish in responding. Too late by moments, it clipped the top branches of the only tree within several thousand square yards, somersaulted itself deep into the heart of the branches with terrible cracking sounds, and did not exit the other side.

Slowly, pieces of it began dropping down, one by one.

A collective groan rose from the wedding party. They started forward with Cochise, whose face took on the look of a stoic who has not quite mastered his philosophy.

Dean lifted a ragged piece. "Here's the tail."

Pam wrapped her arms around Cochise and

kissed him. "Oh, Cochise, that was so beautiful. Thank you. Thank you!"

"Jesus, Cochise," Spider said, squeezing his shoulder. "I'm sorry."

"No sweat, man. She did what she was supposed to, she died in a good cause." He pulled a cellophane bag of rice from his breast pocket. He scattered it over Spider and Pam. "Go on, man! Baltimore's waitin' and you want those daylight driving hours."

Rice came showering from all directions.

Hollering good-bye, Spider and Pam ran for the Nomad. Spider jockeyed the car out from between the other two, backed in a tight circle, laid on the horn, and burned rubber down the road, nose heading due east.

Behind them, the waving and kiss-blowing went on long after they were too far away to appreciate it.

And that is the honest and Gods'-truth story of the Citizens Band, heartland USA. Have a good one today and a better one tomorrow. And may the good Lord take a likin' to ya. We definitely down. We definitely out. We gone.

THE RADIO SHACK GLOSSARY OF
CB TERMS

||||||||||||||||||||||||||||||||||||||||||||||||||||||||||||||||||||||||||||||||||||||||||||||||||||||||||||

The "10" Signals

Code No.	Meaning	Code No.	Meaning
10-1	Receiving Poorly	10-9	Repeat Message
10-2	Receiving Well	10-10	Transmission Completed, Standing By
10-3	Stop Transmitting	10-11	Talking Too Rapidly
10-4	OK, Message Received	10-12	Visitors Present
10-5	Relay Message	10-13	Advise Weather/ Road Conditions
10-6	Busy, Stand By		
10-7	Out Of Service, Leaving Air	10-16	Make Pickup At...
10-8	In Service, Subject To Call	10-17	Urgent Business

Code No.	Meaning	Code No.	Meaning
10-18	Anything For Us?	10-34	Trouble At This Station, Help Needed
10-19	Nothing For You, Return To Base	10-35	Confidential Information
10-20	My Location Is...	10-36	Correct Time Is...
10-21	Call By Telephone	10-37	Wrecker Needed At...
10-22	Report In Person To...	10-38	Ambulance Needed At...
10-23	Stand By	10-39	Your Message Delivered
10-24	Completed Last Assignment	10-41	Please Tune To Channel...
10-25	Can You Contact...?	10-42	Traffic Accident At...
10-26	Disregard Last Information	10-43	Traffic Tieup At...
10-27	I Am Moving To Channel...	10-44	I Have A Message For You (or...)
10-28	Identify Your Station	10-45	All Units Within Range Please Report
10-29	Time Is Up For Contact	10-46	Assist Motorist
10-30	Does Not Conform To FCC Rules	10-50	Break Channel...
10-32	I Will Give You A Radio Check	10-60	What Is Next Message Number?
10-33	EMERGENCY TRAFFIC AT THIS STATION	10-62	Unable To Copy, Use Phone
		10-63	Net Directed To...

Code No.	Meaning	Code No.	Meaning
10-64	Net Clear	10-89	Radio Repairman Needed At...
10-65	Awaiting Your Next Message/ Assignment	10-90	I Have TVI
10-67	All Units Comply	10-91	Talk Closer To Mike
10-70	Fire At...	10-92	Your Transmitter Is Out Of Adjustment
10-71	Proceed With Transmission In Sequence		
10-73	Spreed Trap At...	10-93	Check My Frequency On This Channel
10-75	You Are Causing Interference	10-94	Please Give Me A Long Count
10-77	Negative Contact	10-95	Transmit Dead Carrier For 5 Seconds
10-81	Reserve Hotel Room For...		
10-82	Reserve Room For...	10-99	Mission Completed, All Units Secure
10-84	My Telephone Number Is...		
10-85	My Address Is...	10-200	Police Needed At...

Note: Any 10-code signal may be reversed by stating it as a question. For example, 10-20? would mean "What is your location?" or 10-36? "What is the correct time?"

CB Slang

CBers, like any special interest group, develop a language of their own. Many of the words and phrases you'll hear originated with the truckers and relate to traveling, road conditions and police speed traps. New words and phrases come into use constantly. These that follow are some of the most often used.

Advertising—Police car with its lights on.

Back Door—Rear vehicle of two or more running together (via CB).

Beat the Bushes—Vehicle driving ahead of a group and going just enough over the speed limit (but not fast enough to get a ticket) to bring out any hidden police cars to investigate. Lead vehicle watching for speed traps.

Bear Bulletin—Report on location of speed trap or police activity.

Bear—A police officer. See "Smokey."

Bear Cave—Also Bear Den. Any police station.

Bear in the Air—Police aircraft used to clock highway traffic.

Bean Store—Restaurant or road stop where food is served.

Big 10-4—Very much in agreement; "You said a mouthful!"

Bottle Popper—Beverage (usually beer) truck.

Boulevard—Highway.

Break—Request to use channel, often given with channel number. i.e. "Break channel one-four" (I'd like to make a call on channel 14).

Breaker—Station requesting a break.

Brown Bottles—Beer.

Brush Your Teeth and Comb Your Hair—Radar unit ahead.

Bushel—1,000 pounds.

Camera—Police radar unit.

Charlie—The FCC. Also, "Uncle Charlie."

Chicken Coop—Truck weighing station.

Chicken Inspector—Weight station inspector.

Clean—No police in sight.

Clear—Communications completed.

Cotton Picker—Used in place of any stronger terms. i.e. "That cotton picker just cut me off!"

County Mounty—County police or sheriff.

Cowboy Cadillac—An El Camino or Ford Ranchero.

Cut Some Z's—Get some sleep.

Drop the Hammer—Accelerate.

Ears—A CB radio or the antenna for a CB radio.

Eighteen Wheeler—Any tractor-trailer truck regardless of actual number of wheels.

Eye-In-The-Sky—Police aircraft.

Evil Knievel—Motorcycle rider.

Fat Load—Overweight load.
Feed the Bears—Pay a traffic ticket.
Fifty Dollar Lane—Leftmost or passing lane.
Flip-Flop—Return trip, or "U" turn.
Fluff-Stuff—Snow.
Fly In The Sky—Police aircraft.
Four Wheeler—Any passenger vehicle with four wheels.
Front Door—Lead vehicle of two or more running together (via CB).

Good Numbers—As in "All the good numbers to you." Best regards and good wishes.
Got Your Ears On?—Are you listening to your CB radio?
Grass—Median strip or alongside of road.
Green Stamps—Money.
Green Stamp Road—Toll road.
Ground Clouds—Fog.

Haircut Palace—Bridge or overpass with low clearance.
Hammer—Accelerator pedal.
Handle—Name used on CB radio.
Harvey Wallbanger—Reckless driver.
Holding On to Your Mud Flaps—Driving right behind you.
Hole in the Wall—Tunnel.
Home 20—Where you live. Home town.

Invitations—Police traffic citations; tickets.

Keep the Shiny Side Up and the Dirty Side Down—Don't have an accident.

Land Line—Telephone.
Local Yocal—City police.
Loose Board Walk—Bumpy road.

Mama Bear—Policewoman.
Mercy!—Expletive exclamation.
Mile Marker—Milepost on interstate highways.
Mix-Master—Highway cloverleaf.
Modulate—Talk.
Monfort Lane—Passing lane.

Nap Trap—Rest area or motel.
Negatory—Negative.

On the Side—Standing by and listening.

Pickum-Up—Pickup truck.
Picture Taker—Police radar.
Plain Wrapper—Unmarked police car. Usually given
    as: Smokey in a plain brown wrapper (brown car),
    plain green wrapper (green car), etc.
Portable Chicken Coop—Portable truck scale.
Portable Parking Lot—Auto carrier.
Post—Milepost on interstate highways.
Pregnant Roller Skate—Volkswagen.
Pull the Big Switch—To turn off the CB radio.

Radio—A CB transceiver.
Ratchet Jaw—Overly talkative CBer.
Rig—CB radio; also truck tractor.
Rocking Chair—Vehicle between lead "front door"
    and rearmost "back door" vehicles.
Roger Ramjet—Driver of a car going well over the
    speed limit.
Rollerskate—Small car such as a compact or import.
Rolling Road Block—Vehicle going under the speed
    limit and holding up traffic.

Sailboat Fuel—Running empty.
Seatcovers—Passengers.
Shake the Trees and Rake the Leaves—Lead vehicle
    watch ahead, rear vehicle watch behind.
Skating Rink—Slippery road.

Smokey—Any police officer.

Smokey the Bear—State police.

Smokey's Got Ears—Police with CB radio.

Smokey Report—Report on location of speed trap or police activity.

Spy in the Sky—Police aircraft.

Super Skate—High performance car, Corvette or other sports car.

Super Slab—Major highway.

Taking Pictures—Police using radar.

Ten-four—Affirmative (see 10-code, Appendix A).

Threes—Best regards.

Threes and Eights—Best regards, love and kisses (those "good numbers").

Tijuana Taxi—Police car with lights and identification on it.

Town—Any city, regardless of size. i.e. New York town, Dallas town, Podunk town, etc.

Truck 'em Easy—Have a good trip.

Twenty—Location (10-20).

Twisted Pair—Telephone.

Twister—Highway interchange.

Two Wheeler—Motorcycle.

Uncle Charlie—The FCC.

Wall-to-Wall Bears—Heavy police patrol.

Wall-to-Wall and Treetop Tall—Receiving you loud and clear.

Willy Weaver—Drunk driver.

Window Washer—Rainstorm.

X-ray Machine—Police radar.